SCARLETT RED
In the Shadows
PART 2

a billionaire SEAL story

SCARLETT RED

In the Shadows

PART 2

P.T. MICHELLE

Interior designed and formatted by E.M. Tippetts Book Designs
www.emtippettsbookdesigns.com

To stay informed when the next **IN THE SHADOWS** book will be released,
join P.T. Michelle's free newsletter http://bit.ly/11tqAQN

SCARLETT RED

BY

P.T. MICHELLE

Mister Black swept in and out of my life like a tornado, leaving me twisted up and forever changed in his wake.

And now that my life is finally back on track, I need to move on, despite the many reminders of our time together.

But our pasts are only as far away as the shadows we hide behind, and sometimes those shadows grow darker, converging on the present in the most insidious way.

He is Black: a stealthy hunter and rainbow master.

I am Red: a truth seeker and desire keeper.

Together we are obsession. Passionate colors destined to be drawn together.

NOTE: SCARLETT RED *is meant for readers 18+ due to mature content. This is part 2 of the* **IN THE SHADOWS** *serial. You should read part 1,* **MISTER BLACK,** *before reading* **SCARLETT RED.**

WHEN RED IS ALL I SEE

Sebastian

M *om* yells for me to get the phone from her nightstand, her voice pitched higher than usual as it echoes down the hall. I open my eyes and try to shake the stuffy grogginess from my head. *What phone? Has she forgotten our phone's been disconnected? Stupid medical bills.* I glance at the clock. One-eleven glows back at me. Mom must be getting ready to go to bed. She usually stays up late reading. She claims it helps her escape from the pain. I rub my face and wonder if I dreamed her calling me. Mom screams at the same time I hear the door to our apartment slam on its hinges.

What's happening? I stumble out of bed and run blindly toward my mom standing at the front of the hall. Other than streetlight bleeding through the blinds and casting shadows on the walls, it's dark in our apartment.

A man in a ski mask approaches Mom. "Move," he barks in a gruff voice.

"We don't have anything." Her words are low and shaky. "Even the TV is broken."

I skid to a stop behind her, but she throws her arms outward. She's not letting me past her. "Stay *back*, Sebastian."

I'm big for a seventeen-year-old. The masked man must've felt threatened. He quickly points the gun at me and narrows his dark eyes.

"No!" Mom screams, jumping in front of the gun just as it goes off.

Her slight frame flings back into mine and I catch her. "Mom!" I yell, stunned into immobility. As we fall to the floor together, the intruder empties his gun into us. Heart pounding in fear for my mom, all I can do is clutch her close and jerk with each bullet jolting her body.

I try to yell, to scream at the motherfucking bastard, but nothing comes out. I'm in shock, and all I can do is lay there frozen, while the man turns and ambles out of our apartment like he'd just delivered pizza, not shredded my mother to bits.

Warm blood oozes over my fingers. I don't have enough hands to stop all the blood flowing from her wounds. I crawl over her, gulping my fear back. I try, but there are just too many holes.

You need to dial 911. Get your head on straight! Call. No fucking phone! No neighbor will dare offer help for fear they'll be next to catch a bullet. Mom had said something about a phone in her nightstand. I gently set her aside and run to her room. Dragging open her drawer, I find a small flip phone inside. *Where did that come from?*

I grab it and dial 911. Once I tell the operator where to send an ambulance, I rush back to my mom's side to wait for the sirens.

My heart races as I frown at the phone in my hand, my fingers sticky with blood. *Where did she get this?* Opening it once more, I scroll through to see who she has called. No past history. One number is stored under contacts.

No name. Just a number.

I dial and put the phone to my ear.

"Hello?" A man says sleepily.

"I think I have the wrong number," I say, sounding hoarse.

Just when I start to hang up, the man replies, "Sebastian? Is everything all right?"

I frown, my stomach churning. "Who is this?"

The man sighs heavily. "Is your mother all right?"

"No," I croak, shaking my head. "She's not moving."

The man's speaking but sirens begin to blare in my ear. They get louder and louder until it feels like my eardrums are going to explode. As soon as I yell for it to stop, my eyes fly open.

Exhaling a harsh breath, I scrub my hands down my face, then grab my ringing phone from the nightstand. Five a.m. glows red on the display. "You have five seconds to make this early call worth my time," I growl into the receiver.

"I'm assuming you're Sebastian. I'm detective Bill Danvers. Carl Resinski over at the ninth precinct recommended your firm—well, you—saying you see stuff others don't. We'd like you to come take a look. At this point, I'm willing to pay the damned Tooth Fairy to catch this bastard."

"On behalf of BLACK Security, fuck you, Danvers."

Just when I move my thumb to end the call, the man calls out, "Wait! Sorry, that came out wrong. Listen, I'm at my wits' end on this one. This is the second redhead this year. And two years ago, there was a string of five, same MO. All have been strangled and left naked with bloody wounds and welts all over their bodies. The freak mixes the victim's blood from her wounds with food coloring to make it even brighter before he splatters it all over the scene. His special calling card. We can't allow this guy to do it again. Can you help us out?"

Grunting, I agree to meet him at the latest victim's address in a half hour. *Bright Red.* I can't go a day without seeing that color everywhere and automatically thinking of her. Today's going to be brutal in more ways than one. It's why I hate the gory murder cases the most. *What is Red doing now? I can never get her out of my mind. Has she thought of me even once these past three years?* Shaking my head to clear it, I stand to grab a shower, glad for the distraction from rehashing past regrets.

My dream comes back to me as I step under the hot pounding water. It has been a while since I've dreamed about my mother's death. Too many other nightmares have crowded in since then, filling the dark space and shoving thoughts of her death to the recesses of my mind. Probably dreamed about it due to Mom's cold case file finally making its way to me. I'd requested it from a law enforcement buddy the other day. I mentally step through what I remember and wonder how it'll compare to her file.

After I meet with this detective and survey the crime scene for him, I'll go for a long run to clear my head, then crack open Mom's folder.

CHAPTER ONE

Talia

"*I think* this event at the Hawthorne resort will do you a world of good, Talia."

Glad that Aunt Vanessa's voice is coming through clearly in my laptop's audio connection, I pause in painting my toenails and glance at my computer screen. I've written a full chapter so far. The words are telling a story. But is the story compelling enough? I sigh at my pink toenails, my current form of procrastination. I have three months to get the third book in my suspense trilogy off to my editor. Wiggling my toes, I recap the polish and make sure to direct my voice toward my computer. "You know I prefer going to Martha's Vineyard in the fall."

"You need it now, dear. It's beautiful in the summer. I'll bet you could use a little sun. That's probably why you haven't turned the video feature on. I like to see your face when we talk."

"I haven't turned it on because I'm working." I tap out a couple of nonsense sentences on my keyboard so she can hear me typing.

"Then why am I just now hearing the keys?"

"Because you're distracting me from my job—"

"When I got the invitation for a singles' event, I instantly thought of you." She talks over me as if I haven't spoken. "I insist that you take my slot."

"You should go, Aunt Vanessa. It'll be just what you need." My aunt has been a widow for a year now. She'd married later in life, and in a sad twist of fate lost her husband, George, to cancer just three years after their wedding.

"This is a younger crowd, Talia. Plus, I'm just not ready to get back on the singledom horse yet. Maybe never. Anyway, Charlie keeps me entertained. He wants me to go to a couple of wineries this weekend. He's looking for the perfect wine for Stuart's birthday present."

"Too bad Charlie bats for the other team. You two make the best couple."

"It's so true. He just gets me, warts and all, but this is about you. The Hawthorne event is perfect. According to the invitation Hawthorne sent out, it's touted to be a social series of fun gatherings. No strings attached. Go and release your inhibitions."

I snort. "That so isn't me and you know it."

"That's the whole point, Talia. You need to escape from

yourself. You've been through a lot the last couple years. First the Tribune shafts you, then Nathan's cheating. I'm the only one who has been here for you. The only one who will *always* be here, and I'm pretty sure all that upheaval in your life is why this last book is giving you a fit. You're worried about starting something new. What's next for you once that book is done? Am I right?"

Thanks for bringing past crap up, Aunt Vanessa. I've managed not to think too much about the shambles my life had fallen into before I started writing. "There will always be new mysteries to write," I answer my aunt in a light tone. "Who else can say they get paid to make stuff up all day? This is a dream job."

"You know what I mean. I want to see you more. I want some family time. You're always so busy hiding behind your writing."

Just then the sunlight catches on the solitary diamond on my finger. Shining brilliantly in my eyes, it feels like it's mocking me and backing up my aunt's words. I grit my teeth and spin Nathan's diamond around, closing my fingers around it. "I'm not hiding. I'm on deadline."

"I know your latest book isn't due for a bit now that you got that extension. You have time to take a few days off. You're *going* to Hawthorne. I'll call ahead and let Trevor know you're coming. He's always up for a good time."

"A good time? Are you trying to set me up on a date? Um, no offense, but I'm *not* taking leftovers," I say, swiveling around in the chair to get back to writing.

Aunt Vanessa's laughter floats through my laptop speakers. "I'm afraid Trevor's a bit too young for me. He's in his late twenties, so that makes him perfect for you."

"Is he the resort masseuse?" I tease.

"Trevor's more than that. He might officially be the helicopter pilot for the resort, but since he lives on the Hawthorne property, he's kind of a jack-of-all-trades there, which means he does a little bit of everything from maintenance to security to…well, let's just say I've seen a few ladies take advantage of his well-built services. He's definitely eye-candy."

I inwardly cringe, hoping she won't follow that up with more indirect sex talk.

"Ooh, bow chicka bow wow!" Cass says over my shoulder, making me jump. "Whatever you're trying to convince her to do that involves eye-candy, she's in. Can I come too?"

"Ah, I didn't realize you were there, Cassie. I was talking about sending Talia to my favorite resort, Hawthorne, at Martha's Vineyard, for an extended singles' event."

"I just got back from a grueling shoot." Cass lets go of her rolling bag to flop back onto the sofa, her camera bag still slung over her shoulder.

I watch Cass flip her long dark hair over the couch's arm and blow out an exhausted breath. With her gorgeous hair and light brown eyes, you would think she would be in front of the camera, not behind it. Instead, she's been flying off to Paris, London, or New York doing one photo shoot after another for the last year. With her gone more than she's around, it feels like I live by myself most of the time.

"I'll get you an invitation too. Bring casual and some formal wear. The resort will provide anything else you need for the events."

"Can we get a helicopter ride too? This Trevor guy sounds intriguing."

My aunt chuckles. "I'll see what I can do. There, you see, Talia. Now that your best friend's going, you have no excuse not to go."

As I shoot Cass a you-are-so-dead glare, she gives me an upside-down cheeky grin, then rolls onto her side, calling out in a cheery tone, "She's going. It's escape to the Vineyard time! Thanks, Aunt Vanessa."

CHAPTER TWO

Talia

"*So,* what level panty-obliterating gaze does our pilot have?" Cass breathes heavily into the phone. "Is it disintegrate-at-first-glance level or slowly-melt-away-with-prolonged-heated-stare level?"

My hand grips the phone. "Why are you calling to ask me this? You'll see for yourself soon enough."

"Ummm, you won't believe it!" she squeals in my ear.

"Oh no you *don't.*" I halt dragging my roller bag across the concrete toward the helicopter pad. I recognize that super-excited voice. "Your ass better be in a cab on the way to this airport."

"Well, it's in a cab…"

"Cass!" I hiss quietly. "I knew you having a quick breakfast with Sergio this morning was a bad idea."

"I'm sorry, Talia. He booked Simone and Nicolai for a shoot in Greece, but then his photographer got food poisoning, so he called me. Do you have any idea how much I've wanted to shoot each of these models? And to have both of them together is incredibly rare! I can't pass this up. This could be *the* shoot that puts me on the map."

"You're already all over the map." I look up to see the helicopter pilot glancing at his watch. Great, he's as annoyed as I am.

"Listen, you'd better go without me. Ever since Nathan's betrayal, you've been so out of commission the past year, I'm surprised your crotch doesn't make creaky-hinge sounds when you walk. You do realize that hinges eventually lock up for good if they don't get lubrication, right?

Rolling my eyes, I sigh. "You're ridiculous, you know that?"

"That's what friends are for...and hey, you'd better not still have his ring on. I know you put it on yesterday to remind yourself what an ass he is, but just because he called out of the blue doesn't mean jack. The douche still cheated on you."

She doesn't know Nathan has been trying to contact me at least once a month since I dumped him. Sometimes via text, sometimes email, but his phone call a couple days ago definitely surprised me.

"He's not entirely to blame, Cass. There are things I wouldn't let him do, and I think that complicated our relationship."

I hear a door slam and horns beeping in the background. "As in kinky things?" Cass whispers into the phone, sounding intrigued.

"As in oral sex," I say in a low voice.

"What! Are you crazy? Most women would be happy to let their guys—" She trails off, obviously in a place she can't talk freely. "Why not?"

"I don't know. I just haven't let him."

She snorts. "Apparently you've never had really good oral sex or we wouldn't be having this conversation."

Her sarcastic comment conjures a memory of Sebastian's silky dark hair sliding between my thighs, his powerful hands grasping my bare butt in a firm grip as he slides his tongue intimately along my sex. A warm flush instantly spreads across my skin. God, it's been three years, yet I can still feel the heat of his hands possessively palming my body, the hot moisture of his mouth making me melt like it was yesterday. *Has he thought of me as often as I've thought of him?*

Sebastian Quinn, the one man I want but can never have.

One night with him at that masked costume party was never going to be enough, but sadly it had to be. Sebastian had been too intuitive. He was the type who would never let me keep my past in the past. I need it to stay buried deep. Along with all those memories.

I wanted to look him up so many times, but I never let myself. My willpower to stay away is only so strong. Keeping him firmly out of my sight is my only protective defense, because he's never been out of my mind. Not to mention, it would kill me to learn that something happened to him while he was off on a mission with his SEAL team. Or, slightly less painful, that he's married to a gorgeous wife and has two equally beautiful kids, one of them a charismatic boy with his father's pitch-black hair and dual-colored eyes.

"If you have to think about it that hard, then I'd say the answer is 'no,'" Cass says in a dry tone, pulling me out of my rambling thoughts.

"I *have* had good oral sex," I huff out. "I just wasn't ready for that level of intimacy with Nathan."

"If you weren't ready to go there with Nathan, then you didn't need to be engaged in the first place. I'm so glad you're going this weekend. Let loose, get a bit of sun on that fair skin, and have fun. You need it, girl."

I didn't bother telling her that I have already turned around and am heading back to the terminal, but then a man calls out behind me, "Are you Miss Lone?"

Cass snickers in my ear. "Your aunt booked you under your pen name? How very incognito. Go. Have a blast. I'll expect all the gritty details when I get back. And I do hope it's of the sweaty, dirty talk variety."

"One-track mind," I mutter into the phone, then jerk around when my bag's handle is swept from my hand.

"Is this all you have?" the guy asks in a deep, raspy voice, the kind that brings to mind highway roadhouses, smoky bars, and dimly lit dance floors. Cass would call it, sex-on-a-stick rough.

"My God, that's definitely a panty-dropping voice if I ever heard one. Tell me what he looks like—"

I hang up and tug on the rim of my Fedora, squinting at the dark-haired guy behind my dark sunglasses. "That's me, and yes, just the one bag."

"Where's my other passenger?" He glances around, the sun glinting off his aviator sunglasses and highlighting the thick stubble on his chin that looks to be a couple days away from a full beard.

"Unfortunately my friend isn't coming."

Nodding, he pushes the handle down and picks up my suitcase. I follow and can't help but notice his nicely shaped butt in tan cargo shorts while he stows my bag in the back of the helicopter. The guy must work out constantly if his muscular calves are any indication. He opens the passenger door for me. "You can be my co-pilot."

I glance toward the seat behind his. "I don't mind sitting in the back."

"You get air sick?" he asks, frowning slightly.

"No," I answer quickly and try not to stare at how well his black T-shirt accentuates his sculpted body. His general height and coloring are similar enough to Sebastian's that I feel a pang of regret I never got to see Sebastian's whole face that night in his dark bedroom. Flashes of lightning blocked by tree foliage outside his window only left me with puzzle pieces of his face—his eyes and forehead, his ear and hairline, his jaw and mouth, and the rare dimple in his cheek when he smiles—but never the complete picture to carry around in my memory.

"Good. Ready to take off?"

I nod to clear Sebastian comparisons out of my head. This guy's voice and general demeanor are very different. He's more relaxed and less intense. A beer and nachos kind of guy.

"Then hop in. You'll get a better view up front," he says, waiting for me to climb inside.

Without asking permission, he grabs my seatbelt and leans over me to hook me in. I tear my gaze away from the dark hair flopped across his forehead to focus my attention on the lone scar slashed across the back of his right hand. He didn't get that playing golf. Yep, he's definitely rough-around-the-edges, even if he does take care of his body.

After he buckles me in, he tugs on the belt. "Good and tight?"

I let out a low laugh at his no-nonsense approach. He might not be the flirty Trevor I was expecting, but my aunt was right about one thing. He's definitely eye-candy, of the rough-and-tumble sort. Cass would be elbowing me and uttering panty-obliterating comments under her breath right now. "I'm not going anywhere."

Nodding, he shuts my door then climbs in on his side. Once he's seated, he pushes a few buttons to start the engine and calls over the noise of the spinning blades above us. "Ever been on a helicopter ride before, Miss Lone?"

"No, and call me T."

He smiles briefly, pushing a hand toward me. "Nice to meet you. I'm Bash."

Bash? Everything inside me stutters and my breath halts. *Isn't Bash a nickname for Sebastian?* When I quickly pull my hand away, he slides his sunglasses down his nose and squints against the sun.

"You okay? Are you nervous about flying?"

Two gorgeous bright blue eyes stare back at me—not Sebastian's unique dual chocolate brown and brilliant blue one. The sight reboots my stunned brain, which then goes into major comparison mode just to be sure. Even though Bash is obviously ripped, he's leaner than Sebastian's thick bulk. His eyes are different, and his hair is longish, brushing his collar, instead of close-cropped. Bash has a beard and his voice is definitely deeper and raspier. He's not Sebastian. Disappointed yet relieved, I exhale and try to get control of my nerves. I really *do* need a vacation. "I'm not nervous. So, Bash? As in Bashful? And here I thought you were Trevor, the Not-So-Bashful."

Pushing his glasses back up his nose, he chuckles as he double checks his own seatbelt. "Nope, just Bash. I'm filling in for my buddy. Trevor hasn't taken a vacation in two years."

I smirk. "I heard your buddy has it made at Hawthorne. His reputation precedes him."

His attention cuts my way. Dark brows pull down behind his shades as he picks up his headset."Sometimes we need a vacation from ourselves."

The sharpness in his tone surprises me. Apparently

there's more to his friend than my aunt knows. "I can certainly relate to that," I say, nodding my understanding. Pulling my hat off, I run my fingers through the tangled mass of hair that unravels past my shoulders the second it's free.

"Fucking hell," Bash mutters, drawing my attention. Just as I snap my gaze his way, he turns his sunglasses toward the instrument panel and puts his headset on, then immediately speaks to the airport tower.

What was that about? There's nothing wrong with the helicopter, is there? I quickly scan the panel of lights. *Like there will be a red flashing light with bold, black letters, saying "Caution, about to die," Talia.* With Bash's ears covered by the headset and the engine roaring, conversation without yelling is impossible, so I take solace in the fact he isn't hammering the heel of his hand against the instrument panel to get something working and glance at the hat in my hand.

I'd worn it to provide a bit of cover, along with my sunglasses. In recent months, I'd gained a pretty strong following with my second book's release, but last week, after my agent insisted that I do a live interview with a local TV show, a few people actually recognized me around town. That had been both an exhilarating and worrisome feeling. I'd been spoiled with the anonymity my penname had given me since I sold the trilogy. Did I really want to give that up just to gain more exposure for my series?

As I stare at the hat, it hits me that the TV interview

also explains Nathan's sudden ramped up interest. I'd been so surprised he called the other day that I answered the phone…

"What do you want, Nathan?"

"I want you back, Talia. Nothing happened. I swear."

The picture of that perky blonde intern in the process of unzipping his pants just as I stepped into his office to bring him a surprise dinner flashed in my mind. The thought of what was about to happen made my stomach churn all over again.

Sighing, I rolled my eyes, almost numb to the hurt. "Even if nothing did happen like you claim, it never should've gotten that far."

"She came on to me. I didn't do anything."

I knew he was raking his hand through his dirty-blond hair, its short, bedhead curls flipping around his fingers. He always did that when he was frustrated. I didn't want to think about him at all. Gripping the phone tight, I snapped, "But you sure as hell didn't stop her either, did you?"

"Talia, I miss us. Things aren't the same without you. At the office. In my apartment. In my bed. You're missing. I want to see that gorgeous red hair lying across my pillow. You just need to trust me. I want to be there for you. I can even help you get your job back."

"I quit."

"Not because you wanted to. Listen, let me help. I'd do anything for you, but you never let me. You always kept me at arms length, never letting me close. I realize now that it wasn't me, and that's just who you are—"

"I don't need your help, Nathan," I said, then hung up.

That distant person that Nathan thinks I am, isn't the real Talia. Sebastian is the only one who has seen a true glimpse of me. But the fact Nathan mentioned my red hair confirms that he must've caught my interview on that TV show, because the whole time we were together, he'd only seen blonde hair framing my face.

The helicopter lifting off pulls me from my thoughts. And when no warning lights flash or sirens blare, I relax and settle into the seat to enjoy the view.

Forty minutes later, Bash lands the helicopter smoothly. He doesn't speak as he removes his headphones, then hops out of his side.

While he opens the back door to retrieve my suitcase, I try to unhook my seatbelt, but I can't seem to find the release button. It doesn't help that my sunglasses are too dark now that we're parked in the building's shadow. Dropping my glasses in my lap, I reach for the latch once more at the same time Bash opens my door.

"I'm trying to get it," I say, looking up at him while working to free the latch.

Bash doesn't say anything or move to help. It's like he's frozen in place, his expression unreadable behind his dark glasses. Sighing, I stop moving. "This belt is more complicated than I realized."

He shakes his head, then leans in. Brushing my hands out of the way, he frees me with a flick of his wrist on the latch, his tone gruff. "It's a quick release."

When he steps back, I laugh at my ineptness. "Apparently only if you know what you're doing."

"Those without experience shouldn't be able to free themselves so easily," he says in a clipped tone, crossing his muscular arms.

Suddenly, I feel naked, exposed, like he finds me lacking somehow. I slide my sunglasses back on, then set my hat on my head. "Thank you for the ride over. I appreciate it."

He holds my gaze a second longer, then steps back to pull my suitcase's handle forward. "Welcome to Hawthorne, Miss Lone."

Why is he acting so stiff and formal now? Is it because we've landed on Hawthorne property? I wonder as I climb down from the helicopter. "Thanks."

When I move to take my suitcase, he holds fast to the handle. "You here for one last fling before you're hooked for life?"

For a second I think he's hitting on me, until I follow his line of sight to the engagement ring on my outstretched hand, then the tone of his question sinks in. His obvious judgment ticks me off, so instead of answering, *"No, I only came for my friend and I wore this ring to keep random single guys from hitting on me down to a minimum,"* I say, "Actually, I'm here for some inspiration. I'm an author who writes about asinine pilots." Then I turn and walk into the main building. *Let him wonder what kind of books I write.*

CHAPTER THREE

Talia

"*Miss* Lone, we're thrilled to have you for a visit!" Smiling broadly, the gray-haired man buttons his suit jacket around a middle-aged paunch as he steps out from behind the main desk. Taking my outstretched hand in both of his, he bows slightly. "I'm happy to host you as a special guest to Mrs. Granger once again. I hope your helicopter ride was pleasant?"

You mean other than my temperamental, judgy pilot? I smile at the resort's owner. "The trip over was quick and uneventful, Mr. Hawthorne." I find it amusing that my aunt always books me at the resort, listing me as "her special guest, bestselling author T.A. Lone," and never as her niece. I'm going to have to tease her about how pretentious she's become.

"Wonderful then," he says, nodding his approval. "We've taken the liberty of putting you in the Executive suite in the West wing of the resort. I hope that'll be conducive to some recharging time for you." Patting my hand, he grins. "Of course, over the next several days we have planned activities if you care to join in. I believe you have some romance in your books, yes? At least that's what Patty tells me. There's a listing of all the social events waiting for you on your desk."

Chuckling, I nod. "Yes, romance is a small subplot that runs through my books. Thank you so much. You and your wife are fantastic hosts. I hope it wasn't too much trouble accommodating Delia Chambers in my place last year?"

His hand around mine tightens a bit. "Not at all, Miss Lone. It was just so tragic."

I release his hand and furrow my brow. "What was tragic?"

He blinks for a second as if waiting for recognition to filter through. "Oh, you didn't know?"

"Know what?" I ask, tension edging into my voice.

"That Mrs. Chambers had to be rushed to the hospital for anaphylactic shock after returning from an outing in town. When I called to check on her, the doctor told me they couldn't save her and she'd passed away."

My heart jerks. "Oh no. I had no idea. How awful." I wondered why Delia hadn't emailed me later to let me know how much she enjoyed Hawthorne's last year. I'd given away several big prizes as a thank you to those who'd helped support and run a huge on-line social media campaign when my second book was about to release.

Delia, along with a few others, ran my fan club, and since I had a looming deadline, I drew her name as the winner of my weekend. When I didn't hear from her after the getaway weekend had passed, I just assumed she'd gotten busy with life and hadn't had a chance to email me.

Mr. Hawthorne ushers me away from the desk to stand beside a tall fern, his tone turning to a low hush. "I assure you, Miss Lone, we take every precaution here at the Hawthorne resort for guests with special food requirements, but there's no way we can control what they eat while out exploring the town."

I nod my understanding. "I'm sure you did. No one's to blame. It's just so sad. I had no idea."

Nodding his obvious relief, he pats my shoulder. "We sent flowers to her family, but please, next time just make sure to let us know in advance whenever you send any more guests our way. We'd like to give them extra special treatment if we can."

I tilt my head, confused. "But I did let you know Delia was coming. I spoke to your wife about her."

"Oh, yes." He nods. "I wasn't referring to Mrs. Chambers. I'm referring to Mr. Sheehan."

The name Sheehan only sounds slightly familiar. Was he new to my fan club? I didn't have another weekend at the Hawthorne to give away, so I'm not sure what exactly the owner is talking about. Is he mixing me up with some other author? "Mr. Sheehan? When was this?"

"Yes, Bradley Sheehan. He was here five months ago. He brought in a voucher for a one-night stay, saying you'd sent him. That night he ate dinner here, but the maid said his room looked like it'd never been slept in. That's why I remember. It was so odd that he didn't take advantage of our wonderful beds."

Worry clouds my thoughts, but I don't want to alarm the owner. Not yet at least. Maybe the guy used the name Sheehan once, then switched to an on-line persona later. I have a picture of a fan club meet up that Delia sent me last year in my email. Maybe he's in it. "Do you remember what Mr. Sheehan looked like? Maybe his description will ring a bell. I've given out several prizes this year, so it's hard to keep track." *None of the prizes I gave was another trip to Hawthorne. That was a one-time, unusual circumstance.*

"Donald might remember. He was helping out behind the desk that night." As soon as Mr. Hawthorne waves to a young, floppy-haired bellhop, calling him over, his phone rings. Pulling his phone from his pocket, he says to me, "He'll be right over. If you'll excuse me."

"Of course. Thank you. And I promise to always keep you in the loop in the future."

"Wonderful!" Smiling, he walks away, putting his phone to his ear.

While I wait for the bellhop to finish helping three women, each with two pieces of luggage, I check my phone for a text message from Cass. Sure enough, she'd sent one.

Cass: Mr. Sexy-Voiced Pilot must be hot as hell for you to hang up on me like you did.

Me: You'll never know since you're NOT here. Traitor! You're the only reason I came.

Once I hit send, someone lifts the handle on my suitcase. Turning to address the bellhop, I stiffen. "Where's Donald?"

Bash tilts his chin toward the closing elevator doors with Donald and six pieces of luggage squished inside. "He's going to be busy for a bit. I'll help you with your luggage. You're in the Executive suite, right?"

I push my shoulders back. "Thanks, but I'll just wait for him."

He acts like I haven't spoken, walking across the lobby with my suitcase in tow as he heads toward a long hallway leading to the West wing.

"Hey!" I call out, striding after him when it becomes obvious he's not stopping. "I can take my luggage to my room myself."

"Then why did you need Donald?" he says over his shoulder without breaking his stride.

The hall is too narrow for me to pull up beside him and the suitcase, so I just follow behind, fuming. "Because I want to talk to him about a guest who stayed here before."

He glances over his shoulder, blue eyes flashing at me

before he opens a door at the end of the hall. "Who was it? I might know the answer."

What floor is the Executive suite on? I wonder, following him into the stairwell. "You said you're only here to fill in for Trevor while he's on vacation, so no, you won't know since this pre-dates your time here."

Shrugging his agreement, he lifts my suitcase and starts up the stairs. I climb behind him, silently counting to a hundred to keep my temper in check as we clear several flights. So far we've climbed past the forth floor. Normally I wouldn't mind, but I'm in heels and I'm pretty sure he's taken the stairs on purpose to pay me back for calling him an ass.

Finally he stops at the fifth floor door. I bite my tongue to keep from making a snarky remark about bypassing a whole bank of elevators earlier.

We emerge in a quiet alcove and then walk all the way to the end of the plush, carpeted hall.

"I need to check if your room's ready, Miss Lone."

When he holds his hand out for my keycard, I hesitate. "Isn't that the maid's job?" I say, but hand him my key anyway.

"Stay here."

After he shuts the door in my face, I stand outside, getting more annoyed by the second.

A minute later, he opens the door wide and pulls my suitcase inside, handing me the card back. "You're all good."

"Okaaaaay then." When he doesn't say anything, it

hits me why he's still standing there. "Oh, sorry. Just a sec." I lift my purse and pull out my wallet to give him a tip.

Bash ignores the cash I try to hand him, his mouth tightening. "Listen, I think we got off on the wrong foot."

I slide the money back into my wallet. "No, you were pretty loud and clear in your assumptions about me. Now, if you don't mind, I have a bellhop to track down."

He glances at the clock on the wall next to the door. "Donald has already clocked out and left by now. He's a waiter over at the Bayside Bar & Grill during his off hours. Your questions will have to wait until tomorrow."

Like hell they will. I'll track the kid down myself. My thoughts must've shown in my expression because he folds his arms. "If you can wait a couple hours, I'll take you."

"I'm perfectly capable of taking a cab."

He frowns. "Some of the bars and pubs near the Bayside restaurant attract a rough crowd. It's better if you don't go alone."

When I start to argue, his expression shuts down, stubborn written all over it. I sigh and shrug. It's not like I'm likely to rope anyone else into going with me within the next hour or two. "Fine, if you insist."

Bash holds my gaze for several seconds, like he wants to say something else. My heart thumps fast, and I work hard to keep my face from revealing just how tense I am. The way this man looks at me, his bold stare reminds me so much of Sebastian, it's uncanny.

I exhale a sigh of relief when he nods and leaves without another word.

After I quickly change into a tank top, a lightweight, wide-weave sweater, a flowery skirt and sandals, I brush my teeth, run my fingers through my hair, then shove a pen and notepad into my purse. It's just five o'clock. If I go now, it's too early for rebel-rousers to be out drinking and already drunk enough to cause me issue. If not, the stun gun in my purse will take care of the rest.

I open my door and startle at the sight of someone just outside. Bash is leaning against the wall, arms crossed over his broad chest.

"What are you still doing here?" I ask, my tone sharper than I intend.

"Waiting for you to do something stupid."

Irritated that he'd pegged me so well, I lie. "How is going downstairs to participate in Hawthorne's activities stupid? I'm just doing what's *expected* of me." Without waiting for his answer, I blow past him and head straight for the stairs. At least then I can get out of his line of sight quickly. Waiting for the elevator would allow him too much time to stare at me. The man's just too unnerving.

Why did I ever think he was laidback? Oh yeah, the scruff on his jaw lulled me into thinking he actually relaxes from time to time. Maybe part of the reason he's getting under my skin is because he brings back memories of Sebastian, but the other half is that he seems to see right through me. How *did* he know that I wasn't going to wait for him to take me to Bayside? Do I have stubborn stamped on my forehead?

Regardless, I don't like that he makes my heart race, even when he's being an overbearing ass. That's the last thing I need right now. As soon as I reach the main floor and step into the lobby, a tall, blonde woman close to my age jumps up from a lobby chair, event pamphlet in hand.

"Hi, please tell me you're going to the Oaken bar. I really want to hit the wine tasting in there. We can walk in together." Dressed in an expensive pantsuit and designer flats, she waves manicured nails in the direction of the bar, a waft of expensive perfume floating my way while her confident expression fades somewhat. "This might be singles stuff, but after ending an eight-year relationship, I'm a little rusty at all of this."

I glance down at my sandaled feet and mid-thigh skirt, feeling very underdressed next to her. "Um, well… I'm not exactly dressed for a wine tasting."

Hooking her arm in mine, she smiles, her make-up creasing in a couple of places. "You're fine, darling. I'm Cynthia Drummond by the way. Let's go see what mischief we can get into."

I like her exuberance. She's a bit over the top with her heavy makeup and bright pink lipstick but she seems fun. "You can call me T."

She blinks at me. "As in the wooden thingy a golf ball sits on?"

Laughing, I let her pull me along. "Close enough."

When we enter the bar, a group of eight men and women from their mid-twenties up to mid-thirties are seated around one of the pub's big wooden tables. A handsome blond guy dressed like a Manhattan lawyer is holding court with an empty bottle of vodka.

"Apparently they've decided that vodka was to their taste," Cynthia murmurs with a giggle before she draws me forward to hear what the guy is saying.

"Ladies, welcome! You make us an even ten. Okay, I sent the staff on a wild goose chase for a specific wine, so we could have our own party instead of a stuffy tasting. Everyone grab a shot of vodka," he begins, gesturing to the twenty or so shots sitting on the table. Once we all have one, he says, "For fun," then takes a shot.

"For whatever the hell," I say and drink my shot while Cynthia downs hers in a fast gulp.

Once everyone has taken a shot, he continues, "Now that liquid fire is dancing in your belly, everyone grab another shot and find a seat around the table. Don't drink it yet, just sit it in front of you."

This could get interesting, I think as Cynthia sits down and pulls me into an empty chair beside her.

Mr. Manhattan lays the empty vodka bottle in the center of the wooden table. Grinning, he flashes perfect teeth to go with his neatly gelled hair. "The rules are simple. Spin the bottle. If it lands on someone you'd like to kiss, lay one on them. If you prefer to pass, take the shot in front of you." He lifts a full bottle of vodka. "We'll make sure you never run out."

Hmm, an adult version of Spin-the-Bottle. Okay, I could deal with this. Most of the guys aren't bad looking.

Not that I plan to kiss any of them.

Manhattan goes first, giving the bottle a hefty spin. We all wait to see where it'll land. My heart races as it slows down. When it bypasses Cynthia and me to land on a dark-haired Wall Street banker guy, I snicker at Cynthia's audible sigh of frustration.

Manhattan grunts and takes a shot.

Wall Street smirks. "You'd better have, Grant!"

Grant grunts and sets his empty glass down. While he's refilling it, he nods to the petite brunette sitting next to him. "You're turn, Adeline."

Laughing, she spins the bottle. When it lands on an Upper East Side guy, she giggles then walks over to kiss him. It's clear she intended to just give him a quick peck on his perfectly trimmed goatee, but the dude grabs her around the waist and pulls her into his lap for a proper kiss. She lets him, then smacks his shoulder when he finally pulls back. "Not fair, Jacob."

He shrugs, unrepentant as she makes her way back to her chair. It's interesting to me that all of them seem to have learned each other's first names. How many events have they already attended before I got here?

A lanky guy gets lucky when his bottle points to a well-endowed woman with silky black hair. She lets out a low laugh and curls her finger in a come-hither motion. He eagerly complies, collecting his kiss with bent over, swooping gusto.

The turn shifts to a well-dressed surfer-type with longish, light-brown hair beside Cynthia. Mr. California waggles his eyebrows before spinning the bottle. The moment the bottle slows to a stop in my direction, Bash's voice sounds behind me.

"Mr. Phillips, the front desk requests your presence."

The man stands, his gaze never leaving mine. Flipping his hand, he dismisses Bash. "I'll stop by after this event."

Just as he takes a step toward me, Bash moves in front of him, his arms folded over his chest. "They mentioned something about your credit card not functioning. Immediate response is required."

The man's face turns bright red against his hair. He cuts Bash an annoyed look before stalking out of the bar.

Bash shrugs and sits down in the vacated seat to address the lanky guy who'd spun the bottle before Mr. Phillips. "I was able to fit your round-trip flight into my schedule tomorrow, Mr. Hammond."

While they're quietly discussing departure and arrival times, Cynthia rubs her nails against her palms, eagerness in her vivid blue eyes. As soon as she starts to grab the bottle to spin it, her cell phone rings.

With a heavy sigh, she slides the bottle over to me. "Here, take my turn. I'll be right back."

Why not? Biting my lip, I spin the bottle. It seems to take forever to slow down, but when it finally does, of course it lands on Bash.

My face instantly heats. Thankful he's too busy talking to the guy to notice, I start to reach for the bottle to re-spin it, when several people say, "Ah, ah!" And a couple of girls share their thoughts out loud.

"Are you crazy?"

"Can I have your turn?"

Bash stops talking and glances up to see the bottle aimed on him. He smirks and raises a dark eyebrow, challenge in his bright blue eyes.

The last thing I should do is kiss the man. I'm already strangely attracted to him. All because he reminds me of *someone* else. How screwed up is that? A meaningless fling is not what I want or need right now, despite what my aunt thinks.

So I grab the shot glass and toss back the liquid courage, amid the girls' gasps of shock and extreme disappointment.

Cynthia's reappearance in the chair next to me saves me from having to meet Bash's gaze as I set the empty glass down.

Just when I slide the bottle back to her, saying, "It's your turn now," Bash leaves the room as quietly as he entered.

CHAPTER FOUR

Talia

"*Thanks* for agreeing to take me to Bayside," I say, sliding into the passenger seat of a black, low-slung Porsche.

"You're welcome, girlfriend." Cynthia adjusts the stick, shifting into gear. She grins as she revs the engine, then we take off with a squeal of wheels.

"So what happened after eight years?" I ask as we head toward the waterfront.

"With my guy?"

"Yes, why did you break up with him?"

Her gaze narrows slightly. "He left me to fend for myself one time too many. I realized that if I was ever going to be happy, I needed to take control of my life and become who I wanted to be on my own, without his shadow hanging over me."

I smile. "I'm sure that realization was very freeing."

Her eyes sparkle as they shift back to me briefly. "You have no idea. Going after what I want has been very liberating. It hasn't been easy. I've learned to plan more, to be meticulous in the details. It even brought me here for the 'find a new guy' part of my plan. I never in a million years thought I'd be attending a singles event, yet here I am, a bit nervous but having fun."

My brow furrows slightly. I can't help but think about the bumpy road my life has taken. I graduated from Columbia, full of hopes and dreams, never thinking that my career at the Tribune would be over just as it was getting started. There I was, only a year-and-a-half into my investigative reporter role at the Tribune newspaper, and my fast ride on the corporate bullet train got abruptly derailed. All because a credible informant for the biggest story of my career—a human trafficking operation run out of a strip club—turned out to be a complete fraud. The head editor quashed my story, and before I could find another person to come forward, the whole illegal operation moved on.

Unfortunately, the most influential article I'd produced prior to working for the Tribune was for my college paper, but I'd written it anonymously. So even though I did have some well-received smaller articles under my belt, as far as the Tribune knew, I didn't have any other "big story" credentials to offset my complete and utter screw up.

I would never regret writing that piece anonymously

SCARLETT RED   41

though. In college, I'd been instrumental in closing down a drug dealing and blackmail ring on campus—a win that was equally personal and professional to me. I'd written my article without credit to assure protection of my source, a girl named Mina Blake, an heiress to the Blake empire. Only Mina and my editor knew I was the author behind the article.

Sure I miss helping expose cover-ups and illegal happenings—getting demoted at the Tribune was akin to being blackballed in the journalistic world—but writing novels still lets me solve mysteries. It's just in a different way. Eventually people's memories will fade, but as much as I hope investigative reporting will be an option for me one day, there aren't any guarantees. I mentally sigh and glance Cynthia's way. "But what if, even with all your careful planning, things don't work out the way you want?"

She presses her lips together, then shrugs. "I'll adapt. I've done it before. I can again."

"Flexibility is good," I say, nodding.

"Being versatile is *key*." Pulling her car alongside the curb a short walk from the docks, she cuts the engine. "That's another thing I learned in my gazillion therapy sessions. A plan is only as good as the variables you can control. Multiple plans assure you're prepared for the ones you can't."

As Cynthia gets out of the car and smiles at me with a confidence worth envying, I climb out too. She's not really pretty per se, but she exudes vibrancy and has a shimmering light in her eyes that tells me she won't give up until she succeeds. And isn't that really half the battle in the pursuit of happiness? Accepting who we are and going for what we want?

What do I want? My aunt is right that finishing this last book means I'll have to face the fork in the road that is my future, and I'm not sure which path I want to take. Not a single story idea worthy of writing down has come to me lately. Yet the other path back to helping others through journalism has been effectively shut down for now. Why am I in such a rut?

"Come on slow poke," Cynthia says, waving me forward.

I put one foot in front of the other and lift my head higher. *Screw the non-forkness of my path. I'll plow a new road if I have to!*

"I don't know if this is such a good idea, Cynthia." I eye the stream of men heading into the bar next to Bayside's restaurant with reluctance. Granted, they look harmless enough. Just a bunch of hardworking men stopping by for a beer after work. A few guys close to our age, who were also waiting on Bayside to open in an hour, had stepped into the bar. When the door closes behind the last guy, she grabs my arm.

"Come on, T! It's called Spurred. How fun is that? Did you hear that honky-tonk music? Half the guys who went in were wearing boots. I'll bet some are even dancing. I've always wanted to learn the two-step."

As much as I don't want it to, Bash's comment about the bars around the restaurant bleed into my thoughts. I grip the bottom of my purse, feeling for the stun gun deep in its depths at the same time a Jeep pulls up. While I'm debating, two college-aged girls hop out of the vehicle. Laughing and chatting, they stroll up the wooden steps and past the wicker chairs on the bar's porch, then walk inside as if it's their regular hangout spot.

Straightening my spine, I push my hair over my shoulder and hook my arm in Cynthia's. "Let's go!"

With an old-style saloon feel of rough-hewn wooden tables, chairs and a scuffed-up dance floor, the place is packed with people at the bar vying for drinks. Beer bottles in hand, many have already spilled onto the dance floor, one big mass of moving bodies.

"Looks like you won't be doing any two-stepping tonight," I tease Cynthia.

She shrugs, scoping out all the guys. "The night is young. Let's get a drink."

We make our way through the crowd and approach the bar where I order a beer and she orders a glass of white wine.

"Really?" I look at her and sweep my hand silently to the crowd around us.

She shrugs while we wait for the bartender to make our drinks, calling out over the loud din. "You can take the girl out of the city, but you can't take the city out of the girl."

Just as the bartender puts our drinks down, an arm encircles my waist and some guy behind me nuzzles his scruffy-bearded chin along my neck. "Hello there, Gingersnap."

I turn and push against his chest, disentangling him from my waist. "Back off or this Ginger *will* snap."

He puts his hands up, eyes filled with amusement. "Ooh, she's a feisty one. I'll see you on the dance floor."

I roll my eyes and turn to pay for my drink, muttering, "Dream on."

Cynthia snickers in my ear. "Gingersnap. You have to give him points for originality."

"I don't have to give him anything." I grab my beer and take a couple of swigs. "No one touches me without my permission."

"So prickly. I've touched you many times." She giggles and takes a sip of her wine.

"That's different." I roll my eyes at her as we maneuver out of the bar crowd. Standing along the edge of the dance floor, we enjoy our drinks while watching people dance. Or try to dance in some cases.

"This really is very entertaining," Cynthia says later after we've people-watched for a bit. She's laughing at the obnoxious bearded guy, who just tried the same move on another girl only to get an elbow in the gut.

"See." I point my bottle toward them. "She didn't like being touched either. I'm not prickly."

Cynthia pats my shoulder and we move out of the way

as more people crowd onto the dance floor. "You don't understand what it's like to be tall. Guys try to cuddle up to you because you're small."

"I'm five-seven. That's not short for a woman," I say, finishing off my beer. Setting the bottle on a nearby table, I look up at her. "How tall are you? You can't be more than five-ten."

She nods. "Yeah, but that's tall for a woman. It limits the pool of men who'll give me the time of day."

"Care to dance, Blondie?" A guy with two-day's scruff on his face touches his cowboy hat as he clasps Cynthia's elbow and leans in closer. "Let me show you what good 'ole boys can do on the dance floor."

Laughing, she hands me her empty glass and takes his hand. "Show me what you've got, Cowboy."

I snicker when they get out there and she convinces him to show her how to do the two-step. She glances my way, all smiles, a mischievous look in her eyes.

Setting her glass down, I wave to her to have fun and head for the bathroom. Two shots and a bottle of beer are finally hitting me.

As soon as I leave the bathroom, stepping into the dim, crowded hall full of girls and guys waiting in bathroom lines, a heavy, woozy feeling descends over me.

I stumble into someone and murmur an apology, pushing my hand against my head.

Sudden terror makes my pulse whoosh in my ears. My palms turn damp as I quickly shake my head to clear it. *No, no, no. Not again.* The sense of unrealism shifts the floor beneath my feet. This time feels much heavier, like it's pulling me under. I blink rapidly, heading down the hall as fast as I can. I glance around, fear seizing me as I look for Hayes's leering face among the crowd. Somewhere in the back of my mind, I know it's illogical. The bastard's in prison for drug cooking and dealing, but I can't stop my mind from being sucked into the past, back to the days where my innocence and freedom were stolen from me.

My skin crawls with the feel of Hayes' warm breath rushing across my neck and I hear his voice in my head. "You just need to relax a little." The strong, bitter taste of the powder he brushed across my lips suddenly fills my mouth all over again, making me want to gag.

He's not here. My stomach heaves anyway. *I have to get out of here. Get outside and breathe in fresh air.*

My heart is hammering by the time I make my way past the dance floor and through the mass of people to the bar's front door. I think I hear Cynthia calling me, but I need open space, not people pressing against me. I need to breathe, so I keep moving forward, each step feeling slower than the last.

The second I escape outside I run into someone. The man grips my arms. "Hey, are you all right?" But even though the deep resonance of his voice seems familiar, I can't get the words to form.

His hold on me tightens as if urging me to answer. I open my mouth to say something, but I stumble and pitch forward. With my chin suddenly smashed against the guy's chest, I glance up at the same time Bash looks down at me, a deep scowl on his face.

My world tilts as he effortlessly scoops me into his arms. Pressed against his chest, I clutch my purse to my side, managing a couple words, but his deep voice rumbles against my temple. "Shut up, T. Just be quiet for now. I need to get you out of here."

Why does he sound mad? I try to reason an answer, but my brain just doesn't have the capacity. When he turns to walk off the porch, some guy behind us calls out, "Hey, is she okay?"

Bash pauses, his hands cinching around my body as he turns around to face him. "She's fine."

"Does she know you?" another guy says, echoed by a third man's voice. "She's half out of it, man."

"She knows me," Bash replies, tightness in his tone. I try to get the guys' faces to focus, but they're a blur to me. They sound young, like they're in college. I mumble and wave my hand to let them know Bash wants to help, but apparently I don't sound convincing, because the first guy chimes in again, his tone harder, threatening.

"I think you should just call her a cab."

Bash takes a couple steps and sets me down in one of the wicker chairs, then faces the trio. "I'm not leaving here without her, so I suggest you go inside—"

He's cut off by one of the guys throwing a punch. Bash dodges the fist, then straightens, his voice taking on a steely tone. "I'm going to warn you three just once not to mess with me—"

All three guys go after Bash at once, shoes scuffling and fists flying. When I try to stand and tell them to stop, I just end up slithering to my butt on the wooden floor, the wicker chair digging into my back.

After he slams his fist into one guy's jaw, sending him stumbling back, Bash grabs another guy in a chokehold, then swings his foot back, catching his last attacker in the ankle with enough force to knock him to the ground.

Spitting out blood, hobbling forward, and shaking off grogginess, the revved up men go after Bash again. Everything else moves in a blur before Bash scoops me into his arms and steps over the three, who lay on the porch floor, groping various injured body parts.

As Bash walks down the wooden stairs, my vision starts to dim. After what I just witnessed, I'm pretty sure Bash will keep me safe. Relaxing against him, I stop fighting consciousness and let the encroaching darkness pull me completely under.

CHAPTER FIVE

Talia

$\mathcal{I}$ *stir* the spatula in the runny eggs waiting for them to cook, and just when they start to harden, I reach for the salt in the cabinet above the stove and let out a surprised gasp when a wiry arm appears over my shoulder, grabbing the salt for me. Setting the shaker down on the counter, Hayes bends down from his five-eleven height and says from behind me, "Smells good. Making me lunch?"

My stomach instantly begins to churn. Since Hayes hadn't bothered me in months, I thought he had finally given up on his fascination with me. I still have nightmares about him grabbing me and fondling my boob. My first instinct is to run, but our apartment is tiny. I won't get very far, so I hold my ground, refusing to let him intimidate me.

My aunt's working, but I'm so thankful Walt will be home any moment. I swallow the fear that's scratching my throat raw and force myself to sound tough to the forty-year-old bastard who's standing too close to me. "The door between our apartments is closed for a reason, Hayes. Walt told you to stay away from me. I heard him."

"Why can't I wish you a Happy Birthday? Happened a couple days ago, right? Happy thirteenth, Talia," he murmurs against my ear, his smarmy voice and sickly sweet cologne making my skin crawl. "You're officially a teen now." Hot breath bathes my bare shoulder next to my tank top's strap. "Hmmm, a year older and even hotter."

"You need to leave *now*," I say through gritted teeth, my death grip on the spatula making my fingers numb. While I quake on the inside, I wrap my left hand around the frying pan's handle, ready to use it if I need to.

Hayes moves with lightning speed, snaking an arm around my shoulder.

"Let me go!" I screech.

His forearm locks around my chest and he quickly presses a finger against my lips. "Shhhh!" I try to jerk away, to kick him in that bum ankle he favors, but I'm trapped and unable to move as he slides the thick pad across my mouth. Pushing past my lips, he groans like he's enjoying the moisture in my mouth while rubbing his finger against my teeth. "You need to relax a little."

As he grinds his bulging erection against my butt, the sharp, bitter taste on his finger freaks me out even more. *Shit, shit, shit!* He's just rubbed some of the residue from the Ecstasy pills that he, Walt, and Jimmy package together in his apartment along my gums. Everything inside me goes cold when he continues with a sickening smugness, "It will help you learn to chill the fuck out just like it has Walt."

My mouth begins to tingle and my heart jerks at a frantic pace. When a sinking feeling of inevitability grips me, self-preservation kicks in. I jam my elbow into his ribs and rush to the sink. While I frantically splash water in my mouth, my body heat spikes and my pulse races out of control. Maybe it's not the drugs working just yet, maybe it's my adrenaline making me feel like I'm going to pass out.

I jerk upright at the sound of Walt's key scraping in the lock. Hayes moves close, "Say a word and I'll arrange it so Walt gets caught with a buttload of drugs on him. Go ahead. Do it, little girl. Then I'll have you *all* to myself," he croons before he moves to the open doorway that connects our apartments.

The second Walt walks inside, I want so badly to scream out what Hayes has done despite the threat he just gave, but Hayes leans around the door connecting our apartments as if he's just poking his head in and crooks a finger at Walt. "Come on, Walt. You're here just in time. We've got business to discuss. More just came our way."

Amelia must've heard Walt's name because she comes flying in the kitchen, little arms raised for him to pick her up. "Daddy!"

Walt grins at Hayes and immediately sets the groceries down. Mumbling that I should put them away, he pats Amelia on the head, then walks around her, heading toward the open doorway.

When Amelia tries to follow him, he barks at her, "You're not allowed in here, Amelia. Go watch TV."

"But I want to be with you, Dadd—"

"Go!" he says forcefully. Amelia's blonde hair shrouds her face, but I can tell how much her dad's rejection hurts, so I walk over and swoop her up. "Want to play a board game with me?"

While Amelia pats my face with her little hands, babbling about which game we should play, Hayes looks at me one last time, then chuckles before he closes the door behind them. His smugness leaves me shaking.

Setting Amelia down, I tell her to go find a game, and after she runs off, I stare at the closed door, feeling more disconnected to reality by the minute. *Stupid drugs!* Before I completely lose myself to the buzz, I grab the edge of the counter and sag against it, hissing to the empty room, "Twisted motherfucker!" all the while wishing I'd bitten Hayes' finger off while I had the chance.

A cold wetness yanks me out of my foggy dreamscape, and I blink my eyes open to see a dimly lit Bash leaning over me, pressing a damp cloth to my forehead.

"I don't like it when you don't listen to me," he says in a terse tone.

I quickly jerk upright and back away. Fumbling with the nightstand light, I switch it on and exhale slowly, seriously wondering if I'm losing my mind. For a brief second, in the dark room, lit only by the bathroom light behind him, he'd sounded just like Sebastian.

All dominant and bossy.

Rubbing my arms against the sudden chill washing over me, I realize I'm only wearing my thin tank top and underwear, and my nipples are jutting against the coral-colored material in glaring, hi-beam abandon. I cross my arms over my chest and demand, "Where are my clothes?"

He gestures to the end of the bed where my sweater, bra and skirt lay in a heap. "You were burning up. I needed to cool you down." His serious expression turns hard. "If the wet cloth didn't do the trick, you were going in the shower next. What the hell did you take?"

"Are you serious? I didn't *take* anything. I was drugged!" When he frowns, I rub my forehead trying to remember past the pounding headache. "I had one beer. Someone must've spiked it. It's the only thing I had there."

"You shouldn't have gone by yourself."

I tense at his stiff, angry tone. "I didn't. I went with Cynthia. Oh, shit! How—" I pause and glance around the unfamiliar room to the night sky outside his window. "How long have I been out? If this happened to me...I hope she's okay."

"You've been out for a couple hours. Other than being hot, you were fine. Your breathing only spiked right before you woke up, otherwise I'd have taken you straight to the hospital." He gestures to my phone laying on top of my purse on the nightstand. "Your phone kept buzzing with a few freaked out texts from someone named Cynthia. I finally responded as you, telling her you're fine but had to leave."

I rub my temples, thankful the headache seems to be dissipating. When the air-conditioned air hits my warm skin, chill bumps form. I start to rub my arms once more, then remember my revealing shirt and cross my arms back over my chest. "Can you pass me my clothes please?"

Bash grunts and stands to grab the pile. Handing them to me, he says, "It's nothing I haven't seen before."

"Not mine you haven't," I snap, feeling like an idiot. Whoever spiked my drink must've done it while I was dealing with the guy who grabbed me. Maybe he'd been working with a partner and distracted me while the other person drugged my drink. I should count myself lucky Bash came along when he did. I try to ignore him as I forgo my bra and quickly pull my sweater over my tank top. When I stand to step into my skirt, he doesn't move away. Instead, once I've zipped it up, he steps closer.

Lifting my chin, his expression is hard as granite. "I do have one question. Who is Hayes?"

I swallow and literally feel the blood drain from my face. "Hayes?"

He nods but doesn't release me. "You called him a 'twisted motherfucker.' Call it a hunch, but I doubt you go around using that kind of language all the time."

Blow it off, Talia! I pull from his hold. "He's no one," I say and start to step around him, but Bash clasps my arm.

"T…" When I look up, he turns me back toward him. "Why did you take the shot?"

I blink. "What?"

He moves until his broad chest is almost touching mine. Sliding his thumb along my jaw, he pauses beneath my ear. "Why did you choose the vodka?"

Instead of kissing you?

I've been trying to ignore the tingling each time he touches me, but this time when he applies gentle pressure before moving his thumb down the side of my neck, I burn. Deep scorching heat that shoots straight to my toes.

Before I can think of a proper response, he lowers his head.

Oh, God! He's going to kiss me. This is a bad idea. Right? Despite my thoughts, a jolt of lust curls in my belly, stealing my ability to speak.

His mouth stops a breath away from mine. "Regret it now?"

Frustration and relief war in my head, while desire shoots straight past my chest and vaults to my brain, demanding I press my lips to his. I resist the strong temptation with everything I've got. If I kiss him, I know it'll be for all the wrong reasons. The main one being… he'd just be a substitute for the man I really want.

Why can't I forget about you, Sebastian?

A satisfied smile curls his lips right before he closes the distance. The moment he connects, I take a step back and somehow manage a calm tone while my heart thumps at a crazy, rapid-fire pace. "I think it's best if I go back to my room now. Thank you for getting me out of that bar safely, Bash. I really appreciate it. It turns out you were right. Talking to Donald will have to wait until tomorrow."

I shove my bra and phone in my purse and head for the door. Just as I put my hand on the door handle, Bash says from a few feet behind me, "You think the hired help is beneath you, is that it?"

I turn to him, not liking his assumption or sarcasm. "I've never considered myself above anyone. Ever. Just because you stripped off my clothes while I was *unconscious*, don't presume you know anything about me."

He glances down at my ring hand on the doorknob. "I know enough."

Okay, so I participated in an impromptu spin-the-bottle event, but it was only because he assumed that I planned to ignore his offer to take me to Donald, so of course I had to prove him wrong. Why have I let this man get under my skin? Maybe he should feel some of that itchy burn. "You want to know why I took that vodka shot? Because *there wasn't anything there*. No spark."

He barks out a laugh. "Does the truth *ever* come out of your mouth?" Crossing his arms, he adopts a confident stance, perfect biceps and corded muscles flexing underneath his heather gray T-shirt. "I know chemistry, and you and I, we've fucking got it in spades, sweetheart. Once you're ready to admit I'm right about *that* too, know this...." His brilliant blue gaze slices into me. "When I kiss you, I'll *own* you, and you'll be the one pulling my clothes off."

"Arrogant ass!" I snort. "Do you even *own* a razor?" I don't care that my dig sounds as pretentious as he accused me of being a second ago. The guy has just pushed one too many buttons. Ignoring his chuckle, I start to turn the door handle when he switches to an autocratic tone.

"Don't leave here again without me."

I swivel around, feminine hackles raised. "You're *not* my keeper."

He lowers his arms to his sides. "Have you ever been kept? Really kept?" he asks, his voice quietly intense. "The way a woman like you should be?"

Something in his voice hits me hard and my bones start to melt at a traitorously embarrassing pace. I straighten my spine and speak past the sudden scratch in my voice. "No self-respecting woman would ever let herself be *kept*."

"So you haven't." The pleased purr in his statement, followed by a lion-like curl of his lip kindles the tiny fires flickering through me into a raging blaze. His gaze drops briefly to my left hand. "It has nothing to do with a flimsy promise behind that piece of metal around your finger."

When he takes a step forward, I cinch my hand tight on the handle, ready to bolt, but his mesmerizing voice holds me captive. "It has everything to do with giving yourself over in a complete physical sense. I can show you exactly what that feels like." His focus travels from my face, down my body and back, leaving a singing path in its wake. "And you'll love every aching minute of it."

Why are his words hitting me right in the gut? He's talking like I've already agreed. I shake my head to snap myself out of his hypnotic sexual lure. "Stop trying to seduce me." His sudden dark smile reminds me so much of Sebastian, I grit my teeth and take a deep breath through my nose. "Seriously. Just stop."

"Are you done arguing with me?" he says in a calm, even tone. "Especially after what happened today."

He'd switched gears so fast, I blink a couple times before it occurs to me what he's talking about. He's referring to me not going anywhere without him. "It's Martha's Vineyard for Pete's sake. Today was a weird circum—"

"*T...*" He cuts me off, dogged determination in the stubborn lines on his face.

"*Fine,*" I huff, exhausted from his mental gymnastics. Opening the door, I stalk off to the quiet sanctuary of my room.

CHAPTER SIX

Talia

The moment the sunlight hits my eyes, they pop open. I lay in bed trying to fall back to sleep, but all I can think about is the wildly erotic dreams I tossed and turned to. Every single one featured Bash talking to me about what it means to be his *kept* woman. And even though all he did was talk, I'm laying here in this massive king-sized bed with a painful ache between my thighs, wondering if there's a female equivalent to blue balls. If any man's voice could drive a woman to the brink of sheer sexual frustration, it would be Bash's ultra sexy bass whispering in her ear.

And God, do I ache. Rolling over, I decide exercise may be the only thing that'll expel some of this pent-up passion. If I use the indoor pool now, no one should be around. I'll have it all to myself. The throbbing continues and just as I punch my pillow, my phone rings. Surprised by the early call, I glance at the ID, then click the answer button. "Hey, traitor. Please tell me Simone and Nicolai were worth ditching your best friend for."

"My God, they've been so worth it!" Cass says with way too much pep for such an early hour.

"Don't hold back," I say on a yawn. "Tell me how you really feel."

Cass laughs. "I'm just so psyched to have some amazing shots to add to my portfolio. Sergio liked my shots so much, he booked a couple more shoots while we're here. You uh, don't sound very awake."

"Congrats on more work. And I sound tired because it's six in the morning here." I yawn again.

"Ah, that's right. I always forget time zones. Sorry if I woke you. I just wanted to see how it's going, you swinging single."

I chuckle as I stretch. "Actually, I'm in investigative mode."

"What? You're working on your book? That doesn't sound like any fun, Talia. I told you not to bring your laptop."

"I listen to you about as well as you listen to me." Running my fingers through my hair, I slide out of the massive bed and tell her what happened to the fan I'd sent to Hawthorne and the mysterious second fan who showed up later, while I pull out my laptop and turn it on.

"Wow! Okay, I admit that's sad about the lady, and very strange about the second surprise super fan. I'm sure your mind is going, but please don't spend all your time working. That kind of defeats the whole purpose of why you're there."

"I only came for *you*." I snort while I pull up the photo Delia Chambers had sent me from the themed reader dinner in honor of my last book's New Orleans' setting. Luckily, she'd also provided the names of everyone who'd shown up. Sure enough, Mr. Sheehan was listed among the attendees. Dark-haired with a round, expressive face and a barrel chest, he looks like he's in his mid-forties.

"I really am sorry I couldn't come, Talia. I'll make it up to you. In the meantime, you should take advantage of the social events going on. Isn't tonight supposed to be the masked ball? I was so looking forward to wearing that kickass black dress I bought last month in Paris. You and I together at a masked event again…ah, such fond memories."

"You're not the one who had to cart your drunk ass home," I say as I send the picture to my phone.

Cass *tsks*. "I know you got your very first *some, some* that night, chickie, so don't pretend you don't have fond memories of crashing that costume party. Do you think your Robin Hood actually showed for that coffee date you totally missed the next day? I can't believe you never used your investigative skills to hunt down that man. He was hella hot!"

I haven't tried because Sebastian and I had already crossed paths before I "met" him at the party that night. Eight years before, actually. He didn't remember meeting me during such a dark time in my life, and I prefer to keep it that way.

"We were heading on different paths, Cass. He's probably married with a couple of kids by now," I say in a dry tone.

"Well, this second time around will be even better." She lets out a wistful sigh. "And, now that you're three years wiser, I'm sure you'll totally have the men at that ball on bended knee. Please tell me you brought the gown with the low scoop that exposes your entire back? They're going to drool all over themselves. Promise me you'll take time away from investigating to go. That way I can live vicariously through you."

The pout in her voice tells me she really was excited about attending that event, at least. Of course, it does make me wonder why she prefers fairytale scenarios to real life—even her photography features beautiful people living exclusive and elaborate lifestyles—but I know not to ask. Cass has her own dirty laundry shoved to the back of the closet too. Part of our mutual respect is that we get each other's need to keep our baggage firmly tucked away.

"Yes, I did bring the backless dress. That's one event I thought would be fun to attend." I smirk as I realize that, like Cass, I like the idea of hiding behind a mask. There's just something incredibly appealing about the opportunity to conceal myself in a veil of anonymity, even if it's just for an evening. *God, a therapist would have a field day with me.*

My phone beeps with an incoming message, making me realize I need to start moving if I want to squeeze that swim in before the pool gets crowded. "I'll be sure to make the most of it for the both of us."

"You'd better!"

My screen shows a message from Cynthia responding to my quick reply to her last night when I got back to my room.

Cynthia: Glad you're feeling better. Dancing rocked, but now I need a massage. You must get one! One guy in particular has the BEST hands. ;)

Me: Feeling much better. No massage for me today. Heading to the pool before it gets crowded.

Cynthia: Going to the ball tonight?

Me: Yes.

Cynthia: Finance guy insists we meet for dinner. Might have to miss it.

Me: Reschedule.

Cynthia: I've put him off 3x already. Sigh. TTYL.

Once I reply to a few emails, I put on my black one piece suit and slip into a matching cover-up, then grab my keycard, phone, and a towel and head down to the indoor pool. The smell of chlorine hits me as soon as I walk in, making me smile. It reminds me of learning to swim at the Y when I was in high school. At first I was completely panicked by the idea of water smothering me, but once I got the hang of not drowning, I learned to love swimming as a form of exercise.

I'm happy to see no one around except for a sandy-haired guy stacking fresh towels on a shelf next to a refrigerated cooler full of water bottles. When he looks up at my entrance and calls, "Good morning," I wave and glance down at my room towel with a wry smile. Guess I didn't need to bring one.

Setting my stuff on a lounge chair, I set my cover-up and towel next to the edge of the pool, then quickly dive into the deep end and begin to swim laps. Thoughts of Bash's seductive comments drive me to push myself harder. Only sheer exhaustion will banish his enticing words from my mind. So I let the tug of the water against my body force my mind away from the hungry look in his piercing blue eyes as they slid over me. The cool water helps massage skin that feels too tight along my muscles, while my lungs work hard to keep up with my need to expel him from my thoughts.

I complete twenty laps before the burn in my chest forces me to pause a few feet away from the edge of the pool for more than the quick breath that freestyle swimming allows. When I turn my head, movement in my periphery catches my attention.

The sandy-haired guy is laying a water bottle on my towel. On the thin side, he doesn't fully uncurl his shoulders when he straightens, but he does glance up to see I've stopped swimming.

Looking a bit embarrassed, he offers a shy smile. "You looked like you were working hard. I thought you might want this."

He's around my age, give or take a year. I smile back as I tread water. "Thank you. That was nice of you."

With a slight nod, he backs away. "Enjoy your swim."

Once the main door shuts behind him, I stare at the glistening water bottle, my mouth instantly watering. I want to take a break and down the whole thing, but thoughts of Bash surface once more. I grit my teeth, realizing I'm not tired enough if he can rush to the front of my mind so easily.

Frustrated, I dive under the water, then push to the surface quickly, breaking into the more challenging butterfly stroke as I head to the opposite end of the pool. Two laps later, I'm pretty much wrecked. Panting hard, I'm thankful I'm alone while I perform some kind of weird sideways dog paddle just to make my way to the side of the pool.

I've never been so happy to reach for the edge, but I gasp and jerk my attention up when I realize someone is standing next to my towel.

"That was...interesting," Bash says in a dry tone.

"If that's how you learned to swim, no wonder you're exhausted."

Grrr! Of course, Mr. Too-Fit-For-Words didn't see me doing laps in perfect swim form just a few minutes ago. While he stands there in jeans and a short-sleeved black Henley that shows off his perfect body, his lip quirks slightly like he's trying not to laugh. I instantly bristle. "I'm assuming you're here for a reason other than to judge my swimming ability."

"I am." He leans down slightly and extends his hand to help me out of the pool.

When I frown instead of taking his hand, he raises an eyebrow. "You plan on swimming to the ladder on the other side?"

I might be breathing heavily and my heart is running a marathon in my chest, but the doubt in his tone, the sheer sarcasm flips my stubborn meter. I turn in the opposite direction, and despite every protesting muscle in my body, somewhere deep inside, I find the strength to lift my arms and slice them through the water in smooth strokes. I race across the water, picking up speed. When I reach halfway, I inwardly grin despite my aching muscles. Three-quarters of the way there, my skin starts to feel like it's on fire just before a sharp clenching radiates through my calf, yanking me out of my rhythm. I stop instantly in the deep end, gasping at the fierce agony.

"You okay?"

I barely hear Bash's voice, the pain in my leg is so excruciating. I attempt to massage the spasming muscle, but the water makes it hard to rub it briskly. Plus, I kind of need my arms to stay afloat. I try to flex my heel, but the spastic muscle just won't give. Biting my lip to keep from crying out, I do my sideways dog paddle the last few feet to the ladder. I know I'm not going to be able to climb the metal rungs right away, so I veer to the right of the ladder, intending to grab onto the edge of the pool.

Just as I touch the curved lip, Bash grabs hold of my arm, and I'm pulled out of the water like a toy about to be sucked into the pool's skimmer basket. He doesn't speak, but quickly carries me to a lounge chair and lays me down.

Not that I care. Now that I'm out of the water, my calf is tightening up even more. I try to push him away so I can massage the balled up muscle, but he bats my hands back, snapping, "Stop being so stubborn," right before he grasps my foot and forces it to flex in the opposite direction.

I exhale quickly at the brief relief the flexing provides, but when he clasps the clenched muscle in his other hand and begins to knead the knot, tears finally fall. *God, that hurts like hell!* I've never had a muscle do this to me before. Now I know why trainers always preach the importance of stretching before a workout.

"You could've drowned, all because you're so damned defiant," he says in a harsh tone.

"It's how I've survived," I say under my breath, but he must've heard it, because his jaw muscle clenches and his tight hold on my foot loosens slightly.

I brush the tears aside and watch him focus on his task. The single-mindedness in his gaze and the intensity of his touch surprises me, easing the tension inside me.

"Not defiant. Independent," I correct in a lighter tone. He cuts his eyes my way, eyebrow cocked. "Obstinate."

"Self-reliant." Circling my foot to show him the cramp is gone, I grin. "Thanks for your help."

Amusement flashes in his blue eyes, acknowledging my ironic back-to-back statements, but the humor fades as he continues to stare. Heat suddenly flows through me, and despite the cool air making chill bumps surface on my wet skin, steam simmers just under the surface.

When I glance down at Bash's still hand cupped around the edge of my calf, his thumb slowly slides along my muscle. My breasts instantly tighten in response to the change in his touch. An intended caress.

"Self-reliance can be incredibly unsatisfying, Miss Lone."

His innuendo hits me in the belly and an explosion of lust shoots everywhere at once, making me hyperaware of his closeness and the incredible smell of clean deodorant and all male. I can't decide if it's his words that turn me on or his deeply seductive voice. Either way, I can't let him draw me in. Grasping the chair's arms, I throw my legs over the other side, ready to leave. "I'm all good now. Thank you."

Before I can stand, Bash flattens his palm on the center of my chest and pushes me back against the chair. I grit my teeth, ready to blast him when he says, "I came here for a reason. Don't you want to know what that is?"

I glance down at his hand splayed across my chest, his thumb touching the swell of my breast above the top of my bathing suit, and rely on sarcasm as my first line of defense. "I have a guess or two."

Bash's gaze narrows, and instead of removing his hand, he slides a finger down the center of my chest. Hooking it around the stretchy material between my breasts, he yanks me up so that my face is level with his. "Let's get one thing clear. I don't play games. I'm bluntly honest in my desires. You won't ever have to question if I'm seducing you. Only how long I'm going to make you wait."

Steam curls in my belly, sliding along my veins in scorching trails of want. "For what?" I ask, barely recognizing the huskiness in my own voice.

A confident smile curls his lips. Dark, sinful promises reflect in his eyes before he releases me and stands in one fluid movement. "I stopped by to let you know Donald is here now. I thought you might want to catch him before he gets too busy with the morning rush."

"Oh," I quickly stand and turn my head away, unsure what my expression reflects. I can't decide if I'm disappointed or relieved that he hadn't been trying to seduce me. "Uh, thanks for letting me know."

With a curt nod, he walks away, leaving me standing there shaking from his powerful presence and bone-melting comments.

I quickly dry off, then shrug into my cover-up.

Swooping up the unopened water bottle, I set it back in the fridge before I leave the pool area in a heavy haze of anxious curiosity about the resort's pilot. *So much for ridding myself of thoughts about Bash.*

CHAPTER SEVEN

Talia

"Yeah, that's him," Donald says, his blond hair flipping in his eyes as he points to the picture of the fan club's get together I'd saved as my phone's main screen background for quick access. "That's Mr. Sheehan. I remember because he only had an overnight duffle bag, but he insisted I take it to his room anyway."

"I was told that he'd been gifted a night's stay at the hotel by me."

Donald nods as he leans against the wall next to the elevators. "Yeah, he showed me the signed invitation you'd sent along with the voucher that covered a night's stay and a meal. He was very proud of it."

Tension and excitement thrum through me; I'm finally getting somewhere. "The resort would have a record of the voucher he used, right?"

Donald rubs his brow, deep in thought. "I normally don't work the desk, so I'm not sure what kind of details our system keeps or for how long." He gestures to a girl with straight black hair at the main desk assisting a woman checking in. "Heidi would know."

"Thank you for your time, Donald. You've been very helpful."

After Heidi confirms the voucher was purchased in cash, she calls Mr. Hawthorne for his authorization to approve my next request before she leads me into their office section directly behind the main desk, and points to a door at the end of the hall. "You've got the date the voucher was purchased, so Simon should be able to help you with the rest."

"Thank you, Heidi. I appreciate your help."

I straighten my linen skirt and approach the door marked SECURITY in bold black letters, glad that I'd taken the time to grab a shower before seeking Donald out. Apparently my quest for Mr. Sheehan has turned into a true investigation. Whoever bought that voucher and then later gave it to him in my name should be on the security tape from that day.

A bald man in his mid-fifties opens the door. Smiling, he thrusts his hand out. "Hello, Miss Lone. I'm Simon Maddow. Heidi just called. So you think someone might've impersonated you? Come in and tell me what I can do."

I shake his hand, but pause when I step inside his

office. I'm surprised to see Bash standing by the window, bright sun outlining his fit physique and glinting off his aviator sunglasses. *What's he doing here?* "Oh, I'm sorry. I didn't mean to interrupt your meeting. I can come back later."

"Actually, be glad he's here." Simon waves to Bash, then grabs a laptop from his desk to set it on the round table next to the door. "If we're going to be looking through security footage, this is the guy you want on your team. He has eagle eyes."

Just as Simon opens his laptop and queues up a program, his phone rings. Answering it, he says, "I'll be right there," then gives me an apologetic smile while tucking his phone away. "I need to go meet the ambulance. Someone is passed out cold in one of the lounge chairs at the pool. Probably too much partying last night." Nodding to Bash, he continues, "You don't mind helping Miss Lone out, do you?"

"Not a problem." Bash reaches up to shut the blinds, and the sun is instantly cut out of the room, leaving only the florescent lights' hum above our heads. Coming around the desk, he slides his glasses onto the neck of his shirt and nods to Simon. "Hit the lights on your way out, Simon."

"You're in good hands, Miss Lone," the head of security says. "Let me know if you need anything else, okay?"

As soon as I nod, he smiles and turns off the lights. When he closes the door behind him, the room goes completely dark.

A couple seconds later, my eyes adjust to the low glow coming from the laptop screen as Bash approaches. "Why didn't you tell me someone's been impersonating you?"

I can barely see his face, but he doesn't sound happy. I shrug. "It's not like that kind of thing comes up in regular conversation."

"You and I haven't had a regular conversation since we met."

His dry comment makes me laugh. "Touché," I say, gesturing to the laptop. "Ready to help me check out this security footage?"

"This isn't at all how I pictured getting you alone in the dark," he says, pulling out a chair for me.

His honest comment sends tingles shooting through me, but I pretend I don't hear him as I sit down and move the mouse to stop the screen saver that has popped up.

Once he pulls his chair close to mine, Bash clicks on the security footage folder. "Is this related to what you wanted to ask Donald about?"

I nod, then quickly explain what I'd discovered about the two readers who'd attended Hawthorne resort in the past year. He doesn't say a word until I'm done.

"You really should've told me."

The reprimand in his tone puts me on instant defense. "Why? I barely know you. In case you haven't noticed, I don't trust easily."

"I think getting you back to the resort safely last night should earn me some trust points," he says before turning back to the screen. "What date are we looking for?"

And just like that, he's back to all business. Nodding to acknowledge that he did help me before, I straighten in the chair and give him the date I need.

A couple hours later, we've only made it through the noon footage. I close my burning eyes briefly and arch my spine, pushing my fingers against my back. I'm sure it's sore from crazy pool swimming. "I'll have to get coffee soon." My eyes flutter open as I finish one last stretch.

Bash isn't looking at the screen. His eyes are on my breasts framed by my fitted navy blue halter-top. Lifting an unrepentant gaze to mine, he frowns, "Are you done distracting me?"

Distracting him? Does he think I'm that desperate for attention? Gritting my teeth, I wave my hand. "By all means, let's continue."

He grunts and turns back to the screen. Another hour of footage passes as we watch more people check in. I still haven't seen any of the front desk employees hand a guest Hawthorne's distinctive voucher with the red-berried Hawthorne tree crest stamped on it.

A few minutes later, Bash stops the video. "Did you see that?"

"See what?"

He clicks the mouse to scroll back a few minutes, then hits the play button. I watch the footage, but don't see the voucher I'm looking for. "I don't see anything."

Bash reverses the same amount of time, then clicks play once more. "Watch."

This time, he hits a button that makes the video move much slower. When I start to shake my head, he clicks the stop button, freezing the screen on a frame of the tall fern next to the main desk. "There. Do you see it now?"

I stare at the fern for a couple of seconds before my eyes adjust to what I'm seeing. Someone is hiding behind the fern's fronds. The person can't be more than five-and-a-half feet tall.

I blink at the screen. "How did you even see that?"

Bash smirks and clicks the start button once I nod and we watch the video move forward together. We never see the person in the video, due to a delivery of a huge bouquet of flowers that blocks our view, but we do see one of the desk clerks move to her computer on that end of the desk to speak to someone. Then the clerk types on the computer screen before handing a voucher to someone who's completely hidden behind that bouquet.

When Bash closes out of the video clip folder, I sigh in frustration. "Great. The person who bought the voucher is blocked."

He doesn't say anything as he opens another folder and checks the camera's footage outside the hotel. When I see him sliding the fast-forward to the same time of day, I smile. "Ah, we couldn't catch him inside, but we can catch him entering, huh?"

"Exactly," he says and freezes the picture on a dark-haired, freckle-faced teen entering the resort.

"He's just a kid," I say, surprised. "How are we ever going to track him down?"

Bash shakes his head while clicking through the shut down sequence on the laptop. "We don't have to. I recognize him."

"You do?" I glance his way just before the room goes completely dark.

He clasps my hand and pulls me to my feet. I try to ignore the sensation of his hand wrapped around mine and the warmth of his body just an inch away. "And no, I'm not telling you where to find him."

"Why not?"

He bends close to my ear, his masculine smell wrapping around me like a warm seductive blanket pulling me into his charismatic space. "It's the only way I can guarantee I'll get you all to myself."

"You don't have me," I say, annoyed at the huskiness in my voice. *Why has my body decided to betray me whenever he's near?*

His warm breath, smelling of mints and orange juice, slides along my jaw and up my cheek, stopping so close to my mouth, I feel the mint's coolness on my lips. "I haven't tried yet, sweetheart."

Firm fingers settle at the base of my spine, tugging me against his hard body. "Are you ready for me to begin?"

Why haven't you? I want to scream as sexual tension roars through me, but instead I quickly step out of his hold and say in an unsteady voice, "Please take me to this kid."

His low chuckle sounds a few steps away just before he opens the door. "Then let's go find your impersonator.

After you, Miss Lone."

As he gestures for me to go in front of him, I set my jaw, irritated by the smug satisfaction in his tone and walk past him without a word.

"Nice car," I say while he pushes the button to fold back the Mustang's convertible roof.

"Yeah, Trev does all right here."

Buckled in, I retrieve my sunglasses from my purse and slide them on, enjoying the feel of mid-morning sun on my skin. The weather is perfect. Not too hot or cold. Once we pull away from the resort, I stare up at the few white clouds in an otherwise clear blue sky and inhale the briny smell of ocean permeating the air. "It really is beautiful here. It's sad that the couple other times I've visited I haven't explored beyond the resort, so thanks for taking me. Where exactly are we going?"

He turns onto the main road and flashes a smile. "We're going to West Tisbury. I've seen the kid trying to sell his caricature drawings to guests outside the resort before Simon ran him off. He's actually pretty talented. I have a good idea where I can find him keeping himself busy."

I study his profile, trying to decipher his mood behind his dark sunglasses. "So tell me how you spotted him behind that plant. Simon was right. You do have an eagle eye. I wouldn't have seen that if you hadn't slowed it frame by frame."

"Do you know what Stereograms are?"

"You mean the 3D pictures? I have a really hard time

seeing them."

"A lot of people do. I see them instantly."

I nod. "Ah, now that makes more sense. It's like your vision is hyper-focused."

He lets out a low laugh. "I guess you could say that."

Tilting my head, I eye him. *Did I detect some self-deprecating sarcasm?* "So what do you do when you're not filling in for buddies in need of vacation or kicking bar guys' asses? Where did you learn to fight like that?"

"A gang tried to recruit me when I was a kid, so I've been in a few fights."

"Did you join the gang?"

"No." He glances at me briefly. "What do *you* do when you're not writing a book?"

"I perform odd swimming techniques and accept rides with complete strangers while on investigative adventures," I say, offering a wide smile. When he snorts at my non-answer, his mouth twitching upward, I nod. "Your turn."

Laying his wrist along the steering wheel, he stares at the road. "I own my own asset protection business."

"Asset protection?" I furrow my brow. "As in finances?"

He shoots me a sideways smile. "Sometimes."

"That's not vague at all."

He shrugs. "That's pretty much it, asset management. I have a few employees. The business is growing. I'll expand later, but right now I'm satisfied with the way things are going."

I open my mouth to ask more about it, but his phone rings.

He glances at the screen. "Sorry, I need to answer it." Putting the phone to his ear, he smiles and his tone completely lightens. "Hey! How are you doing?"

Who is this person in his life that makes him light up like this?

No sooner did the thought enter my head then I see his hand instantly tighten around the phone. "He's been in the hospital all of what? Five minutes? Okay fine…two days. Why is she selling it?"

Whoa, that's a quick change from friendly to cold.

Pausing, he pulls the phone away and glances at the screen, then puts it back to his ear, his tone settling somewhat. "That's her calling. No, I'm talking to you right now." A pause. "Should you be doing that? Get the others to help you." Another pause. "Why don't you just send it to me at the resort. I'm here for a bit longer." After he rattles off his room number at the resort's address, he asks, "Are you feeling okay now? Good. Don't over do it. Better yet, make your mom do all the work since she's the one selling. Yeah, yeah, I know how she can be. Just don't let her push all the work off on you." Another pause, then he's back to smiling. "That's just how I'm wired. Someone has to look out for you. Let's get together when I'm back in town."

"Sorry about that," he says, setting the phone into a slot in the console. "Family stuff."

"I'm sorry someone is sick." When he looks at me in

confusion, I clarify. "You said someone's in the hospital."

"My father just had his appendix removed. He's fine now, but while he's out of commission my stepmother has decided to sell the family beach house. My pregnant sister is there clearing stuff out, while I'm sure my stepmother is piling on more work."

"I don't detect any bitterness at all," I say, offering an empathetic smile.

"My stepmother is *not* my favorite person."

His phone rings again and this time, he swears before he answers. "I figured you'd be calling. Honestly, I'm surprised it took you this long. Ah, camped out on your lawn, did they?" A devious smile tilts his lips.

I can't believe the difference in Bash's tone. A sharp edge of condescension mixed with pure dislike. It must be his stepmother. Obviously she picked the wrong guy to get crossways with.

"Probably because I told my lawyer to take care of it last week, making it a matter of public record. Screw the tabloids. I *signed* the deal three years ago, but I just now got around to filing it. Go ahead, show it to him. I don't give a damn about the agreement. I never did. Tear it up if you want."

When he pauses, I cringe at hearing her screech through the phone, *"You're such a manipulative son-of-a-bitch."*

Bash calmly speaks over her shouting. "It's done. You may as well get used to it." Then he hangs up on her. Two seconds later his phone starts to ring again, but this time he turns off the ringer. A few more seconds pass, and his phone must've been set up to read texts out loud, because the automated voice says, "Message from New York area code. 'You must not care about him at all. He'll hate you for this.'"

I gasp when Bash grabs the phone and throws it as hard as he can into a field of sunflowers as we zoom past.

When he sets his jaw and continues to drive like he didn't just chuck a thousand dollar phone into a flower field, I say, "You ah, want to talk about it?"

His aviator-covered gaze swings toward me. "Just family BS. I'm sure you deal with it all the time too."

I look out at the passing farmer's fields. "Not phone-tossing worthy."

"Are you saying you get along with your parents all the time?

"My mom died when I was a baby and my dad's not in the picture."

He blinks at my comment, sympathy taking over his own anger. "I'm sorry. You don't have any siblings?"

Amelia's sweet cherub face and blonde hair comes to mind, but when I try to picture the details of her features, I can't. My eyes suddenly water at the realization. I'm losing my memories of her. *Why did all the pictures have to burn in that explosion?* "My younger sister died when she was little."

"I'm sorry."

I nod and lift my head, letting the wind dry my eyes. "It's just me and my aunt. We're very low key. Never any drama."

He snorts. "You can have mine."

His wry comment takes the edge off my dark thoughts about Amelia's death. "Your sister or the family drama?"

"The drama." He grins. "I'll keep the sister."

I snicker. "I think I'll pass. If tabloids are involved, it sounds exhausting."

"It is."

Nodding toward the windshield, he says, "We've got about five minutes until we get to the festival grounds where I'm pretty sure this kid works. Do you have any enemies from your past who would try to impersonate you?"

When I shake my head, he continues, "What about your readers? Have any of them acted strange or displayed any kind of obsessive or stalker-like behavior?"

"No, none of my fans have been stalker-like that I'm aware of. Yes, they're excited and supportive of my books, but they respect my privacy." I furrow my brow, thinking further back in my past. "For a few weeks in college, not long after the story broke in the school paper about a professor using his authority over students to blackmail them into dealing drugs for him, I felt like I was being followed while the internal investigation was undergoing."

"Why would someone follow you?"

"Because I was the 'anonymous author' of the story. In the article, I alluded to a certain well-loved professor who was involved with the drugs. I gave enough info so that anyone who went to school there would know whom I meant. Needless to say, once the story came out, students started coming forward. I wrote the piece anonymously to protect my source, whom I never gave up. Only my editor and my source knew I wrote the article, but I'm sure some suspected it was me."

We pull in front of the festival's main gates and park in the gravel parking lot. A few hundred people are spread throughout the festival's grounds, children running from game to game, cotton candy or ice cream cones tight in their hands. Among the press of people, huge park rides rise up like odd-shaped towers. Bash and I walk past the center of the amusement park, beyond many big rides, then pass through the food and carnival games section until we reach an area along the back fence, where several artists are sketching drawings of people or painting elaborate temporary tattoos on their customers.

Bash bends close to my ear. "I'll take the lead on this." Before I can discuss strategy with him, he walks over to a thin, straw-haired boy of about ten who's helping customers flip through a book to pick the art they want before they get to the tattoo artist's chair.

"Hey, kid," Bash calls.

"Yeah?" the boy says, eyeing Bash's tall height.

Bash hands him a twenty, then points to an empty easel with a caricature drawing of an old man on it. "Can you go get the artist who drew that for me? I recognize his work and would like to talk to him."

The boy's attention darts between Bash and me before

he quickly pockets the twenty, then nods and runs off.

"He won't be back," I say, expelling a sigh.

Bash crosses his arms, adopting a confident stance. "Yes, he will."

I laugh and pull a twenty out of my purse. "Bet you the twenty you just lost."

"I didn't just lose—" He stiffens, then relaxes. "You're on."

After twenty minutes pass, I look at Bash and hold out my hand. He just grunts and walks over to the artist the boy had been helping. "Do you know where the kid who was helping you earlier went?"

The guy with pockmarked skin and a long black ponytail pushes his hair over his shoulder. "His shift ended thirty minutes ago. He won't be back today."

When Bash jerks a glaring look my way, I manage to hold back my laughter, but I can't keep from grinning.

Annoyed, he addresses the artist as he points to the empty easel. "Where is the kid who owns that stand? I'm trying to find him."

The tattoo guy's dark brown eyes narrow in suspicion. "What do you want with him?"

Bash waves like it's no big deal. "Just to ask him a couple of questions."

I notice we've started to draw attention among the artists lined up along the back gates. Many have glanced up from the their work. Just before I say something, a big hulking guy, his brown hair cut in a bowl style, speaks in a very deep voice behind Bash. "He's not here. You can leave now."

Bash turns from the artist to address the tall guy, who has to be almost seven feet. He's massive. "We're going to stay and enjoy the festival."

The giant clamps a beefy hand on Bash's shoulder, his face folding into a scowl. "You would've bought a festival bracelet. I don't see you wearing one, so you need to leave."

Tension grips me when Bash grabs the guy's massive hand and yanks his grip away from his shoulder. The next thing I know, he has the big guy's arm twisted behind his back. "I'll leave when I'm ready to leave," he says in a hard voice.

"Wait!" I touch Bash's arm, pulling him back. Something about the giant's face had snagged my attention. Taking off my sunglasses, I step around his huge body to stare into his face. No facial hair whatsoever. My God, he's young! Like twelve-years-old, young. Apparently, this kid happens to reside in a body that can crush a car.

"What's your name?" I say to the hulking boy, holding my hand out.

He shoots Bash a dirty look, but when he looks back at me, pink floods his cheeks, even as he folds his oversized hand around mine. "I'm Howie."

I can barely get my fingers to touch either side of his wide palm to shake it. "Hey Howie. My name is T.A. Lone, but you can just call me T."

"Hey, T." When Howie nods while continuing to hold my hand, I smile and gesture to the empty easel. "Can you help us find your brother?"

Releasing my hand, he grins from ear-to-ear, green eyes full of excitement. "I can't believe you guessed that Hank and I are brothers. No one ever guesses that!"

I smile back. "Can you please ask your brother to come talk to us? He's not in trouble or anything. I just need to ask him something. In exchange, I'll be happy to pose for one of his drawings and sign it. Then he can auction it off however he wants."

The big guy's eyes widen. "Are you famous?"

I hold my pointer finger and thumb close together. "Just a little popular, but one day, I hope to be a huge bestseller. I'm an author and I'd really like Hank to draw me. I'd love to use his drawing as my online avatar. Can you please tell him for me?"

I barely finish my sentence before Howie runs off into the crowd and disappears behind the Ferris wheel.

"How'd you know?" Bash asks, appreciation in his voice.

I turn to him. "Know what?"

"That they're family."

I nod toward the artists who've resumed their work now that the excitement has died down. "I think this whole artistic group considers each other family. I saw a couple of them send signals, I think to tell others to warn Hank. But the way Howie came barreling over here... well, only a very close relative does that."

"Or those who've become like brothers during extreme circumstances," Bash says, sounding a bit nostalgic with an edge of sadness.

He didn't mention any brothers earlier. Is he talking about close friends? Did he lose some friendships? He must still be close to Trevor. I don't know anyone else who works another guy's job just so he can take a vacation. The sun shines through Bash's aviators, allowing me to hold his gaze. I smile. "That too, I'm sure."

While we wait for Howie to find his brother, Bash lets a boy, who's walking around juggling three throwing balls, rope him into playing a knock-the-milk-bottles-off-the-stand game. Twenty-five dollars later, Bash hands me his prize with a wry smile: a black beaded necklace worth about two bucks.

"You do realize you just got taken, right?" I tease, putting the necklace on as we walk away.

He lets out a manly grunt. "It's a matter of pride."

"Can I really draw you and you'll sign it?" A teen boy says off to my left, snagging my attention. He's a couple inches shorter than me, but judging by his deeper voice, he's at least fifteen.

I smile and walk over to sit in the chair next to his easel. "Will this be all right?"

Nodding, he sets a narrow wooden box on the edge of his easel and pulls out a couple of charcoal pencils, his dark blue eyes already assessing my face. "What did you want to ask me?"

I watch Bash take up residence behind me and fold his arms, leaning against the festival's gate, then I turn back to wait until Hank begins sketching to speak. "A few months ago you purchased a voucher from the Hawthorne hotel."

When Hank starts to deny my statement, I raise my hand. "You're not in trouble. I just want to know who sent you to the hotel to buy it for Mr. Sheehan?"

Hank's attention strays to Bash as if he doesn't quite trust him. I get it. Bash can be intimidating when he wants to be. "He's okay, Hank. I promise."

Hank shrugs, then resumes his drawing. "A woman just showed up at my easel one day. She asked me to go to Hawthorne and purchase the voucher in that man's name. She gave me a piece of paper with typed out instructions."

"A woman?" I say, cutting a surprised look to Bash. "Did the paper have a hotel crest or special markings on it in any way? Do you still have those instructions?"

"No crest, just plain paper. And no, I tossed it," he says right before he begins to speed through the drawing, a talent that only comes from years of practice. Pausing, he gestures to my hair with his pencil. "She had red hair like you. Though hers was darker, more brownish red. And she was a bit taller."

Anxious, I lean forward in my seat. "Did you know her? Or recognize her from somewhere around Edgartown or here in West Tisbury before?"

He shakes his head. "No. I've never seen her before. She came to my easel late in the day when the sun was almost down and asked me to buy the voucher at Hawthorne. She gave me cash to pay for the voucher and promised a couple hundred bucks." Rubbing his nose with the back of his charcoal-covered hand, he continues, "I got the first hundred for buying the voucher and the second hundred when I delivered it to her."

"Where did you meet her to deliver it?" I ask, hoping that location might narrow down the pool of candidates some.

He swipes his pencil across the page a couple of times as if putting finishing touches on it. "She came back here a few days later to pick it up. I've never seen her here before or after that. Honest, I promise."

A couple minutes later, he says, "I'm done," then steps back from his drawing. "I um, kind of switched it up a bit."

He didn't draw me in caricature like I expected. Instead, he'd drawn a lifelike picture of me. Actually, he'd made me far prettier than I really am, but hey, if I'm going to have this as my avatar, it may as well be a supermodel-worthy rendition.

I take the pencil he offers and scrawl out my fancy T.A. Lone author signature in the corner of his masterpiece. "This is fantastic, Hank. You really are very talented." Handing him the pencil back, I take a picture with my phone so I can create an avatar later.

Once I put my phone away, Hank says, "Can I ask you why you're asking about a voucher I bought for some guy?"

I nod. "I asked because this mystery woman who came to you sent that man the voucher inside an invitation as if it were from me."

His eyes widen and his face pales slightly. "I'm sorry. I didn't know she was going to do that."

Bash steps into place beside me, his stance more relaxed. "If someone offers you too-good-to-pass-up money to do something for them, I guarantee you, it's not for anything good."

When Hank grimaces in guilt, I pat his shoulder. "You didn't know. So what are you going to do with your drawing?"

"What kind of books do you write?" he asks, eyes lighting up.

I smile. "I write mystery."

A wide grin spreads across his face. "I'm going to hold onto it. I just know you're going to be a big name one day."

Laughing, I shake my head. "I don't know about that."

He rocks on his heels, his eyes sparkling with confidence. "Yeah, you will. The way you found me. All this investigating you're doing. I just know it."

"Well, thank you for the vote of confidence, Hank. And for the cool new avatar. If you keep drawing like this, I think you're well on your way to becoming famous yourself one day."

When Hank gets all choked up and turns to rub his eye, mumbling about dust, I step up and grab the pencil again, saying, "And since you're keeping it…" I add a note above my signature, then hand Hank the pencil.

"To Hank, the best artist in Martha's Vineyard,"

Howie reads my note out loud, pride in his booming voice. "Told you she was smart *and* pretty." Grinning, he slaps his brother on the back, sending Hank stumbling forward a couple of steps.

Once Hank recovers and turns to high-five his brother in agreement, Bash says in a bone-meltingly low voice meant just for my ears, "I couldn't agree more."

CHAPTER EIGHT

Talia

"*What* are you going to do with the information you learned from Hank?" Bash asks as he pulls into a shaded parking spot at the Hawthorne resort.

I glance his way as he cuts the engine and sets his glasses on the dashboard. He appears relaxed, but my gut tells me he's far from it. "Since all I have is Hank's description of a tall redhead and no name to go on, the best thing to do is follow the lead I do have. Once I get a hold of Mr. Sheehan's contact information, I'll ask him how he got the invitation."

Resting his wrist on the steering wheel, he turns to me. "Can't you just get that information from the front desk?"

I shake my head. "Since everything was paid for, he

never had to provide any personal information."

Bash frowns slightly. "Do you think it's possible Mr. Sheehan met with this woman who bought him the voucher? That she actually pretended to be you?"

I mull his question for a couple of seconds, my stomach twisting at the idea. "I hadn't thought about the fact she might've actually impersonated me in the flesh, but now that you mention it, it's oddly coincidental that she resembled me so much."

He thrums his fingers on the dashboard as the wind starts kicking up, blowing his hair away from his face. "If he rented a car while he was here, I should be able to get his information. I know the people who run the rental car companies. What's his full name?"

"That would be great." Opening my purse, I jot down Bradley Sheehan on a piece of paper. "Hopefully I can get to the bottom of this before I leave in a couple of days. I really don't like the idea that someone might be going around impersonating me."

When I hold the paper out to him, he clasps my hand along with the paper. "Have dinner with me tonight."

My gaze snaps to his. We'd worked well together to get the information I needed. He didn't have to help me, but he did. Would it be such a bad thing to have dinner with him?

"Hey, Bash!" Two California bleach blondes wearing short tennis skirts walk behind his car, rackets resting on their shoulders. The shorter one arches a perfectly plucked eyebrow. "Care to give us some pointers?"

He glances up at the darkening sky, then smiles at them. "Better make it a quick game, ladies."

"Aw, you can do better than that," the tall, thin one says suggestively before they both laugh and turn down the path that leads to the tennis courts.

When his gaze swings back to me, my pulse jumps and surprise shoots through me. Bash has a dark brown spot in the upper curve of his left iris. I'd never noticed it before, since we've mostly been indoors and whenever we've been outside, he'd worn shades. Until now.

Shoving the paper into his palm, I pull my suddenly shaky hand away from his hold. "I have work to do," I say, and quickly grab the door handle.

Just as I push open the door, he grips my hand once more. "I'd like to spend more time with you."

All I can think about is Sebastian. How he'd ruined me for all men. Nathan had been a bandage. One I thought I could slap on, and with enough time, he would heal the gaping hole Sebastian left behind after our one mind-blowing night together.

I shake my head and pull free once more. "I'm sorry, Bash. I just don't think it's a good idea."

His brow furrows, frustration evident. "It's a fucking perfect idea and you know it."

I step out of his car and shut the door, feeling as if I owe him some kind of explanation. Yes, the chemistry is there "in spades" as he put it. He doesn't deserve this. "You remind me too much of someone from my past."

When I start to turn away, he demands in a low tone,

"Was it that good? Or that bad?"

"Both," I answer honestly, then walk away as thunder booms overhead.

On my way to my room, I get a text from Nathan.

Nathan: I want to talk to you. It's important.

Me: Talk later.

Nathan: Need to talk now, but you're not here.

Ugh. He must be at my apartment. What could be so important?

Me: I'm out of town. Will call when I return.

Once I get back to my room, I don't even turn on the lights. Instead, I instantly strip and head for the shower. Miraculously I manage not to cry while I let the hot water wash away the festival's dust clinging to my sun-kissed skin.

I automatically pick up the bar of soap, but then put it back. The same with the shampoo. By the time I've towel-dried my hair, the storm is raging outside. Thunder rocks the floor and lightning illuminates the room in a strobe-light effect. A heavy wall of rain rushes against the window, its fury thrashing against the glass.

I walk over to my suitcase in the darkened room and slip on a pair of clean underwear, then I unzip the extra compartment in the suitcase and pull out a folded jacket.

My fingers trace over the supple expensive leather before I slide my arms inside and sigh at the brief arousing feel of the coat's lining rubbing against my bare nipples. I tug the cushioned high-back chair over to the window and sit, glad the sheer curtains give me privacy but allow some light in the otherwise dim room.

Leaning against the chair's side arm, I tuck my knees against my chest and push my nose into the jacket's leather collar. Inhaling deeply, I exhale a sigh of relief that it still smells like Sebastian. Well, the seventeen-year-old boy he was when he gave it to me that night in the pouring rain eleven years ago. I've always been careful not to use perfumed products right before I slip into his coat. His smell has faded over time, but I would hate for the leather to lose the unique masculine scent completely.

I've taken Sebastian's jacket with me wherever I go, but it's only when I'm feeling particularly alone that I pull it out. Today definitely qualifies.

"Why can't I let you go?" I whisper as silent tears fall. I know fundamentally why, but it has been three years since I felt his touch. One would think I would've moved past the pining stage by now, that I shouldn't let one person occupy so much space in my head.

Protector, benefactor, lover...my obsession. That is what Sebastian has become.

And now that I've met a man who could possibly push him to the back of my mind and make him a distant memory, I'm sitting here alone in the dark, wearing his jacket. How fucked up is that?

I sigh toward the ceiling and clasp the coat tighter around me, letting the constant rush of the rain outside work its magic on my mind that doesn't want to settle.

Closing my eyes, I listen to the steady beat against the glass and allow myself to embrace the memory of the night I lost my virginity to the only man I've ever fully trusted. The only man I completely submitted to in heart, body, and mind. My skin flushes as I mentally summon the feel of his hands on my skin, the intensity of his gaze and strength in his possessive hold.

During that masked party, I'd given him the name Mister Black before I learned his real name was Sebastian. I rub away my tears and soak in the deep resonance of his voice calling me "Miss Scarlett". Telling him to call me Red later that night in his bed had been my way of revealing that he'd already met me eight years before as a young troubled teen. He'd called me Red back then after he'd given me his coat to keep me warm. Scarlett and Red are the only two names he knows me by.

I never told him my real name, but I'm not sure how long I could've held out if we'd continued our passionate encounter beyond that one night. He'd been too damn good at making me submit to him in ways that should embarrass me, but with Sebastian, they just felt intensely natural. A man with that much power over my body and mind is beyond dangerous to someone with dark secrets. I've stayed away from him physically since then, but now, for my own future happiness, I have to mentally distance myself as well.

"One last time, Mister Black..." I whisper into the storm-darkened room. Settling farther into the chair's deep cushions, I slide my hand up my thigh and fully indulge in every single Sebastian memory and fantasy before I have to let him go once and for all.

CHAPTER NINE

Bash

"*Fuck!*" I slam the heel of my hand against the steering wheel after she walks away, her gorgeous red hair swaying against her back. Thunder rumbles overhead, and as I push the button to close the convertible's roof, I can't believe how she can continue to deny the connection between us.

It was good and bad.

What kind of bullshit answer is that? What happened to make her so afraid to acknowledge what we both know is true. Our chemistry is off the charts. It's so intense, I had to keep gripping the damn steering wheel so I wouldn't reach over and touch her the way I want to. The way I know she wants me to.

I lean my head back against the seat and run through

our day.

I knew she was smart, but I had no idea just how intuitive she is. Watching her at the festival had been both awe-inspiring and arousing at once. Her compassion is heartening, but her obvious intelligence only makes me want her more. I lost count of the number of times I got hard.

A mystery writer. Who fucking *knew*? But after today, I can see where her passion for chasing down a story comes from.

I don't like discovering that someone might've been impersonating her, and it bothers me that I don't have a clue who this mysterious redhead is. At least we have this Sheehan guy's name to check on. Not only will finding out his contact information help her investigation, but it'll be another excuse for me to seek her out again.

Damn, I enjoyed our banter, and though I can tell she still holds a lot back, we're not that different. But it's like she has blinders on. Why doesn't she look closer? Is she really that afraid of what she'll discover?

I pull the keys out of the ignition and fist them in my hand. One thing she'll quickly learn is that I don't give up whenever I go after what I want. And I *want* her so much I can taste the passion between us already.

I got to truly see her today, and now I'm done letting her refuse to see me.

CHAPTER TEN

Talia

I jerk awake at the sound of my phone ringing. Groggily, I stumble in the dark toward my purse on the console table by the door. Flipping on the light switch, I grimace at my rumpled appearance in the decorative wall mirror as I grab my phone.

"Hello?" I say, while finger combing my hair that the chair had completely rat-nested.

"There you are!" Cynthia says, her voice oozing with excitement. "I texted you three times! I wanted to pop by and tell you all about the guy I met earlier today. He's taking me to dinner in a half hour."

I give up attempting to fix my hair and move over to my closet to pull out my dress. "I thought you had a business meeting tonight."

"We finished early. I'm just waiting for my date to pick me up."

"Ah, I see. You'll have to tell me all about it tomorrow."

"Tomorrow? But I have a bottle of champagne and wanted to celebrate with you."

"Well…" I glance outside and frown at the darkness. The storm must've left dark cloud-cover behind. "What time is it?"

"It's eight-thirty. You've got half an hour before the masked ball starts. This could be your pre-party apéritif, as the French would say."

"Eight-thirty! I'm sorry, Cynthia, but I have to take a rain check on the champagne. I took a nap and overslept. I still need to get a shower."

"All right, then. We'll catch up tomorrow, yes?"

I feel bad. I can hear the disappointment in her voice. "Absolutely. And you can tell me all about your hot date."

"You know I will. Go get on your fancy dress and shoes. You're going to be the belle of the ball!"

I give a very unladylike snort. "I doubt that. I don't have double Ds or platinum blonde hair."

"Make sure your dress shows off some leg, and you're golden."

"I'll miss not having my wing-girl. Have fun, Cynthia."

"Always. Talk tomorrow."

Forty-five minutes later, I run my hand along the smooth French twist in my hair and weave the black-jeweled stick deep into the twist to secure it. Using the mirror, I survey the spaghetti straps and low-scooped back that drops all the way past the base of my spine. Even though the dress is black, its clingy material necessitated a pair of barely there, G-string underwear.

As I turn around to inspect the modest scoop neck in the floor length mirror on the door, the thigh-high slit up the right side reveals a lot of leg and a gorgeous, strappy metallic five-inch heel. The sexy shoes are so tall, I had to sit down to buckle the delicate straps at my ankles or risk falling over.

Once I dab on a bit of tinted lip gloss, I check the rest of my makeup. The light line of kohl around my eyes is more than I usually wear, but still understated compared to many of the girls I've seen over the past couple of days, including Cynthia. I slide on the gorgeous, glittery black mask the hotel included with the social itinerary they'd provided, then take one last look in the mirror. I finally look presentable.

Grabbing my small metallic clutch purse, I slip my ball invitation and phone inside and head down to the main floor. My stomach flutters as I approach the ballroom. I know it's ridiculous considering I turned Bash down earlier, but a part of me hopes he might make an appearance tonight.

I'm a half hour late, so the ballroom is packed with three hundred or so impeccably dressed men and women in custom made tuxes and sleek designer gowns. Even the perfumes and colognes smell of rich decadence. The combination is more than I'm used to and a bit dizzying.

"Welcome, Miss Lone." Patty Hawthorne approaches.

Clasping my hand, she beams. "I'm glad you could make it. This is always our most well attended event.

"Thank you, Mrs. Hawthorne." I touch my mask and smile. "How did you know it was me?"

She pats her perfectly coiffed white hair, her cheeks rounding out with her sweet laugh. "I'm a redhead but went white early. We redheads must stick together, dear."

"Redheads unite!" I hook my arm in hers and let her escort me toward the dance floor.

Once we reach the outskirts of the dancing crowd, she asks, "Do you have your clues? It was on the back of your invitation."

I quickly pull out my invitation and turn it over. Three things are typed on it: Red, Black, and Water.

Smiling, she sweeps her hand toward the people dancing. "Okay, the dance will be switching soon."

"Switching?" I look at her in confusion.

She bobs her head. "For the first couple of hours during the ball, every few minutes you'll switch dance partners. The clues on your invitation are specific to male guests here at Hawthorne. Two of the clues might match several of the guests, but all three should only match one guest. If you find the male guest who matches all three within the two hours, you don't have to switch partners any more.

"At that point, you can continue to dance with him, go over to the bar and get a drink together, whatever you like. The goal of this fun event is to try to match-make our guests based on the answers they gave to the survey.

And even if you don't ever find the man who matches all three, you'll have met several other interesting male guests in the process."

Survey? Ugh, Aunt Vanessa must've filled it out for me. I can't even imagine the type of guy I'll end up with. I force a smile. "That sounds…interesting."

Mrs. Hawthorne's eyes twinkle. "I knew you'd love the mystery of it. While you're chatting with your dance partner, work in those clues. I'm sure a woman with your deductive skills will find your match in no time."

Glancing around, Patty stops a man with longish, light-brown hair as he's about to step on the dance floor. "Got your clues memorized?"

When he nods, she tugs him toward me. "Here's your first partner."

He grins and takes my arm, guiding me through the crowd. As his hand settles at my waist, I smile and say, "That wasn't awkward at all."

Laughing, he pulls me into a dancing position and we begin to move to the music. "I regret that I didn't get a chance to kiss you the other day, but at least I can dance with you now. Your dress makes the wait worth it."

"So you like black?" I ask innocently, enjoying Mr. California's harmless flirting.

He shakes his head. "I prefer red, but with your gorgeous hair, black is the perfect contrast on you. How about you? What's your favorite food?"

"Actually it's a spice. Care to guess?"

Just when he starts to answer, the announcer speaks

into the mic, "Switch," and I'm quickly swept into another man's arms.

I manage to work in all three clues with each of my dance partners for the next forty minutes, but none of the dozen men I danced with had the answers to all three of my clues. Granted, six of them were convinced *I* matched all three of theirs. So much for the accuracy of Patty's match-making method.

Overall, the men had kept their questions pretty clean. A few tried to get a little too personal with me, but I made sure they saw the engagement ring on my hand. For the most part, I enjoyed the challenge of working the clues into our conversation. Some dance partners made it easier than others, but I felt a little thrill each time I managed to get the answers to all three questions back-to-back.

As soon as the announcer calls, "Switch", my next dance partner doesn't approach me straight on the way the others had. Instead, I'm quickly turned around, and before I even get a chance to meet his gaze, he steps into my personal space, pressing his body to mine.

I don't care that he's wearing a custom tux worth more than my car. I instantly stiffen and try to pull back, ready to tell him to back-the-hell-off, but I freeze when he splays a hand against my bare lower back and bends close, his voice a smooth husk in my ear. "So we meet again, Miss Scarlett. Or should I say Miss Red? When, in this lifetime, were you going to tell me who you really are?"

Oh God, Sebastian? *Sebastian.* He's here, of all places? The music is drowning out the resonance, but is the roughness in his voice anger? A layer of heat quickly replaces the initial wall of ice that gripped me. My skin instantly flushes in response to his nearness, his solid build, and arousing cologne. Especially where he's touching my back; my skin is humming. Of course, he would choose now to reappear in my life after I've cried myself to sleep saying goodbye to him. *Holy shit!*

"Why are you here?" I whisper in a harsh tone as I pull back to stare at his smooth, angular jaw and black mask.

Even as his hand slides higher along my back, pressing my chest to his, he keeps his gaze straight ahead and begins to move us to the music. "I'm here to find my match." He briefly snaps his gaze to me, his tone lowering. "Though you and I both know the answer to that question." His outstretched hand constricts around mine, his warmth sending a shiver of excitement down my spine. "Why didn't you meet me at that coffee shop like we'd planned?"

I grip his hand on my waist as I stare at his tense jaw. "It's hard to explain. Didn't you get—" I start to ask if he received the box I gave his sister to give to him, but the metallic feel of a watchband underneath my fingers draws my attention. He's wearing the watch I'd left in Mina's safekeeping until he got back to the States. "Your sister told me you were leaving. That you were about to be deployed."

He grips my waist with both hands as we continue to dance. "You know I'm a SEAL?"

I nod. "Mina told me the next day."

His hands tighten around me. "You've kept in touch with my sister all this time, but you didn't bother to contact me?"

The low growl in his tone instantly amps my growing edginess. "No, I haven't kept in touch with her." But now that he has the watch, he knows that he and I had met back when he'd sneakily slipped that very same watch into the leather coat he'd leant a freaked out thirteen-year-old. "How did you recognize me tonight? When we were together three years ago, my hair was blonde."

He tilts his head and smirks, running a finger along my jawbone up to the bottom of my mask. "The bottom half of your face is very unique."

I push his hand away. "No, it's not, Sebastian. Why are you here?"

He clasps my hand and turns it over, pressing a soft kiss to my palm. "I want you to finally tell me your real name."

Every nerve ending in my body quivers from the heat of his mouth on my skin. "Why now—"

"And I want that next day and night we never had together."

I'm so turned on my knees almost buckle. I can't believe he's here, staking his claim on me all over again, as if the past three years never happened.

"Switch!" the announcer says over the mic, making me jump. Sebastian turns to the man approaching us on my left, and says in a lethal tone, "Fuck off."

"That was unnecessary!" I say in a low voice once the guy throws his hands up and walks away, looking for another dance partner.

"Do you think for one minute that any of these men are your true match?" he says smoothly.

If we're so match-worthy, why the hell didn't he come after me? Yeah, I know my annoyance is irrational, but if he's going to act all intense and possessive after three years of radio silence, I should be allowed some illogical thoughts myself. I'll bet he came to Hawthorne like all the other single rich men, looking to get laid. But instead, he happened to see me across the room. Random coincidence at its finest.

Sebastian's arrogance makes me want to punch him, so I glance around the room, scoping out other guys while he slowly spins me to the music. "Oh, I don't know on the matching thing. I've barely scratched the surface here. The night's still young."

"Red, Black, and Water." Sebastian lists the three clues as if he were reading them straight from the back of my invitation.

"How...did you know?" I blink, completely thrown.

He shrugs. "They're my three favorite things."

I tense in his arms. "Just because my card happened to have all three of those items doesn't mean—"

"Aren't you glad I found my razor, T?" He turns so his mask isn't blocking my full view of his eyes. Two bright blue eyes stare back at me. Except the left one has a spot of brown.

CHAPTER ELEVEN

Talia

"*Bash?*" I whisper, my steps faltering. That sense of familiarity I just couldn't shake had been right all along. I want to bitch slap myself for discounting what I knew in my gut, but ignored. I straighten my spine, fury whipping through me and try to stop dancing, but his grip tightens as he continues to move us to the music. "Why the hell were you pretending to be someone else? What kind of mind-fuck game have you been playing with me?"

Sebastian releases a low, sarcastic laugh. "You wrote the book on hiding behind aliases. How many are you up to now? Scarlett? Red? *Miss Lone*? At least I'm consistent in my duplicity."

"Consistent?" I say, trying not to let my voice get too high. All the things he'd said to me as Bash—Every.

Seductive. Word—flashes through my mind. I'm so pissed even his tight hold can't keep me from resisting. I stop dancing and glare at him. "How is pretending to be someone else *entirely*, consistent? I'd love to hear your answer, *Bash?*"

He shrugs. "It was just easier to *not-be-me* while I filled in for Trevor. Bash is a nickname my Navy buddies gave me. It kind of stuck. That's what they all call me."

"Is Trevor a SEAL too?"

Sebastian nods, then narrows his eyes. "You made sure to meet up with my sister, but you couldn't take the time to meet me for coffee?"

"You're mad at *me?*"

When I just gape at him, his tone hardens. "Three years aside, have you considered the fact that maybe I should be ticked that you didn't recognize me as Bash?"

I had gone to meet him at the coffee shop that next day, but I ended up staying out of sight once I overheard that he was getting ready to go off on a mission. Even then, I only saw his profile. "Once you removed your mask in your bedroom that night, the lightning never shined on your whole face, so I never saw it. But despite the changes in your eyes and voice since then, I told you that you reminded me of someone."

His jaw flexes. "And in all this time you never once tried to look me up?"

Even though he'd framed it as a question. It's a statement. The brief hurt in his eyes knocks my righteous anger down a peg or two, but then I lift my chin high. He has no idea how hard it was for me *not* to look him up. "Neither did you, so we're even."

When he doesn't contradict my statement, but just stares at me, tension in his jawline, I sigh. "It just occurred to me. You never did say. What *is* Bash's last name?"

"Black." Irony flashes in his eyes, his lips quirking slightly. "Consistency, Miss Lone."

He'd taken on the name I'd given him that night at the party as his alias? When my stomach begins to flutter, I fold my arms, refusing to be drawn in by his seductive skills. "Are you really here to help Trevor?"

He rolls a shoulder. "In a manner of speaking. I'm helping here while he does some work for me. If he likes the job I've given him, I'll bring him on board as a member of BLACK Security."

BLACK Security? *He named his business Black?* Before I can dwell too much on that mind-blowing tidbit, I tighten my tone to keep myself focused. "Security? You said you protect assets."

"We do. Among other things," he says, trailing his fingers lightly down my arm.

I can't believe he thinks I'm just going to ignore his deception over the last couple of days. I pull away from his touch. "Is there *anything* you said to me as Bash that wasn't some kind of half-truth?" Before he can answer, I expel a sigh of disappointment. "I was really starting to like him."

He stiffens as if I've slapped him, bright blue gaze sharpening. "Bash might've told you he wanted you, but he'd wait for you to come around. And we both know that never would've happened. I know that isn't what you want." He steps close until his chest touches mine. I hold my breath, hoping he can't feel my heart thudding like I've run a marathon. "You want to relinquish control. For me to make you come until you beg me to stop. *Me,* not Bash. If that makes me a bastard for wanting that time back that you walked away from three years ago, I don't give a damn."

He clasps my hand and twists the ring on my finger. "Before you commit yourself to some asshole who doesn't know jack about taking you to places you've never thought you'd go, I want you all to myself. Not for hours. For the rest of your time here."

While my insides rev at the thought of days in Sebastian's bed, he slides his fingers along my jaw, then thumbs my chin upward, forcing me to look at him. "Will you give me that time we lost? I've never wanted anything more." His hold tightens slightly against my cheek. "Let me show you what it means to be owned by your desires. To be fully kept, by me."

Fully kept? He thinks I didn't give myself to him completely before? Granted, he has no clue that I've never forgotten him, or that he's buried so deep in my thoughts, I might as well have a "sole property of Sebastian Quinn" tattoo on my ass, but what else could he possibly have done to make me fully his? The burning question and erotic possibilities turn my insides to mush.

But all the desire in the world can't push away the

anger still simmering. Nothing about his arousing declaration changes the fact he's lied to me for two days straight. He knew who I was, and yet he'd pretended that he didn't. "Why didn't you say who you were once you recognized me?"

When a stubborn look settles on his face and a muscle begins to jump along his jaw, I realize he's not going to answer. "Fine." I start to walk away, but my sandal's buckle suddenly gives way, pitching me sideways into a dancing couple.

"I'm so sorry," I say to them just as a strong arm encircles my waist.

"I've got you," Sebastian says against my ear.

Balancing on only one good stiletto, I don't have a choice but to let him lead me out of the crowd. Sebastian doesn't say another word, other than to press me to his side once I take off the broken sandal. Instead of letting me walk on my tip-toe across the dance floor, he lifts me a few inches and carries me off the dance floor like I'm a life-sized, standup poster.

With no seats to be found in the ballroom, he carries me outside and past the elevators to an alcove with a potted plant and a console table.

"This will have to do," he says. Setting his mask on the table, he holds his hand out. "Lean against the table and I'll refasten it for you."

I set my mask beside his, then hold the shoe up to inspect it. "It's probably broken." It turns out my shoe isn't damaged at all. Apparently I hadn't done a very good job pushing the tab through the tiny buckle. Wishing we could've found a couch or a chair so I could do it myself, I sigh and hand him my shoe.

When I lean against the table and raise my foot up for him, Sebastian lifts the hem of my dress at the open slit and then tucks the material in my opposite hand resting on the edge of the table. "Hold this out of the way."

Grasping the hem, I try not to think about how much of my leg is exposed. Instead, as Sebastian kneels down on one knee, I stare at his close-trimmed black hair. It's back to the way I remember. Then I allow my gaze to wander over the expensive tux stretched across his broad shoulders. The man really is both massive in size and striking in his devastating good looks. He's so damn hot, I want to smack the top of his head for lying to me these past couple of days, then kiss him for just being freaking real and not a figment of my imagination.

I bite my lip when Sebastian runs the pad of his thumb along the arch of my foot, his warm fingers folding around the edge in a firm hold. The angry part of me wants to tell him to hurry up, but the twisted part of me that has never let him go silently begs me to enjoy every second of this.

He hesitates like he's waiting for me to pull away, then he applies even more pressure along my arch. Shivers dance across my skin, and I have to work hard to remain relaxed in his hold. Let him think I'm not affected.

When he slides my shoe on and quickly buckles it, disappointment makes my chest ache. "Thanks," I say and start to lower my foot from his knee, but his warm fingers encircle my ankle, holding me in place as he continues to stare at my foot.

"I didn't tell you who I was, because you'd already rejected me once. Why would I give you a chance to do that again?"

Rejected him? What is he talking about? "I don't understand—"

"Don't talk." His fingers cinch around my ankle, then relax. "Just listen."

Sliding his thumb along my shin, he firmly massages my calf muscle with his fingers. "When you didn't recognize me, as much as I didn't like it, it also occurred to me that Bash had an opportunity with you that, for whatever reason, I'd blown."

He must be talking about the fact that I didn't meet him for coffee. Damn! "Sebastian, that's not what—"

He grips my calf muscle tight. "Let me finish."

Exhaling, I clamp my lips shut.

His grip eases and his fingers trace higher, sliding behind my knee. "You were different with Bash, and I've always wondered if my...intensity scared you away."

Folding his thumb around the bend of my knee, he traces small circles on my sensitive skin. "I need control. It grounds me. I can't explain it beyond that." He releases a low, self-deprecating laugh. "I've never had to explain myself to anyone before, but for you, I'll try."

His declaration melts away my anger. *I would've lied for two days straight too if it meant spending time with you, Sebastian.* I can't help myself. I slide my fingers into his silky hair.

He tenses, then exhales sharply. Moving his hand higher, he clasps my thigh in a possessive hold. "I wanted to know what it would take to get you to open up. I thought that Bash could strip away all your reservations, but the more time we spent together, I began to hate the bastard."

"Why?" I ask, my fingers sliding free of his hair.

He jerks his head up, bright blue eyes boring into me. "The Bash you were getting to know would be too soft with you. Too careful. Too fucking restrained. And that's not me. When it comes to sex, the real me is gritty and intense. Using kid gloves isn't what I want. Nor is it what you need."

My breath whooshes out of my body. I swallow and try to regain control of my voice. "How do you know what I need?"

His fingers dig into my thigh, inching higher. "Because you gave yourself to me that night. You trusted me without question. Why did you do that and then walk away?"

I wish I could tell you, but my past is too fucked up. I shake my head. "I don't know."

His lips twist. "Liar." Before I can say anything, he plants a kiss along my inner thigh. This time, I can't control the gasp that escapes. I'm throbbing hard, aching deeply inside and wanting him so much that I grip the edge of the table and breathe out his name.

"Mmmm," he says, then pushes my dress out of the

way. The moment he sees my G-string, he lets out a deep groan. "Fuck me! You're trying to kill me."

"No, I'm not," is all I get out before he dips his head and slides his tongue along my sensitive, exposed skin, making me shiver in anticipation.

Gripping my thighs in a firm hold, he says, "Say yes to us," in a hoarse voice before tracing his tongue down the G-string's narrow material. Dipping inside my sensitive folds, he follows the length of the material in a slow, tantalizing tease, but doesn't move it out of his way.

"Don't stop," I whisper desperately.

He lifts his head, desire turning his eyes a deep turquoise blue. Determination flashes in them briefly as he reaches for my left hand. Before I realize what he intends, he slides the diamond ring off, his possessive gaze snapping to mine. "This goes while you're with me." Once he pockets the ring, his hands move with determined purpose, sliding under my dress and along my hips. Snapping the edges of my underwear with a swift twist of his fingers, he says, "I can't wait to devour your sweet pussy. I've missed your arousing taste."

While he pockets my underwear, my brain tries to re-engage and remind me that we're in a public place, even if we're mostly hidden, but his hands are already working their magic, tracing purposefully along my thighs, and my body is too amped to care.

Sebastian grips my hips in a dominant hold, but instead of diving in like I expect him to, he takes his time with slow torturous kisses, meandering his way up my inner thigh. He might say he wants this, but his measured control is infuriating.

I thread my fingers in his hair once more, breathing heavily. "Don't you dare make me wait this time!"

Warm breath rushes across my leg, punctuated by a decadent chuckle. "I'll do as I please, and you'll love every second of it."

"Arrogant." I huff my frustration.

"Confident," he counters, pressing a lingering kiss to the tiny triangle of red hair between my legs, so close to where I want him most. "Such a beautiful sight," he murmurs in his deep baritone, rubbing his nose in the patch of hair. Glancing up at my face, he scans the tendrils that have fallen from my French twist. "You have no idea how much seeing your real hair color turns me on even more. Scarlett red is a perfect description." Lowering his mouth to my body once more, he exhales his warm breath intimately across my sensitive parts. "Best damn sight all night."

"You can *sight-see* later," I pant, digging my fingers into his hair and tugging slightly.

"*Hands*," he commands, jerking his head up.

"Really?" I sulk, but comply with his curt nod, telling me to put them back on the table.

He flashes a pleased smile then dips his head. The second his mouth brushes fully against my sex, his tongue sliding deep, a man steps around the corner. I push at Sebastian's shoulders at the same time the guy registers us, then quickly averts his gaze. "Oh, sorry!" Pivoting in the opposite direction, he mumbles, "Got turned around getting off the elevator."

That curly dirty-blond hair! Recognition instantly dawns and horrified embarrassment grips me. I quickly pull away from Sebastian and adjust my skirt, hoping like hell he didn't get a good look at my face—

"What the fuck!" Nathan raises his voice as he strides back around the corner, hands clenched in tight fists. Gesturing to Sebastian, who's straightening to his full six-four height, Nathan's voice raises, echoing in the small alcove. "How many times did I offer? And here you are, *in public*, giving it up to some spoiled meathead—"

Before he can say another word, Sebastian grabs his tie and dress shirt and yanks him against the wall, growling in his face. "Watch your mouth or you'll find out just how hard this spoiled meathead can hit. You don't deserve her. You *never* did."

Worried that Nathan is angry enough to say something stupid and set Sebastian off, I tug on Sebastian's arm. He towers over Nathan, his wide shoulders and muscular strength dwarfing Nathan's medium-build. "Let him go, Sebastian."

Sebastian shoots me an annoyed glance before his fingers ease from Nathan's clothes.

The moment he's released, Nathan jerks his shirt and tie straight and scowls at Sebastian. "I need to have a private conversation with my *fiancé* if you don't mind."

"Ex-fiancé," I correct him, not even bothering to look in Sebastian's direction. As Bash, he'd made one too many assumptions about my reasons for being at Hawthorne. *Did he really think I was here for a last minute fling? Pffft.* He didn't deserve the truth about my engagement. Sebastian didn't give me a chance to tell him.

Nathan frowns. "I'm working on that."

"Obviously you failed in key areas," Sebastian says in a smug tone.

I shoot Sebastian a murderous glare at the same time Nathan calls him a "fucking son-of-a-bitch" and takes a step toward him.

I put myself between the two guys and address Nathan in a detached, matter-of-fact tone. "What are you doing here?"

Tearing his furious gaze from Sebastian, Nathan takes my hand and pulls me a couple steps away. "I came to talk to you about a time-sensitive opportunity—" He pauses and gives Sebastian a pointed look over my shoulder. "Alone."

When Sebastian doesn't move, but instead crosses his arms, a determined look on his face, I sigh. "Can you give us a moment, Sebastian? He's obviously here for something important."

Sebastian's gaze on Nathan's hand around mine is so intense, I honestly worry he's going to go after my ex again. Just as I pull my hand away from Nathan's hold, Sebastian turns his back on us and leaves.

The sense of panic that grips my stomach scares the hell out of me, but I force myself to remain calm and not think too hard about Sebastian walking away. I can only deal with one testosterone-enraged guy at a time. When I turn back to Nathan, it feels odd to be eye-to-eye with him, but also empowering. The spiked heels' height gives me an extra boost of confidence. It's the first time I've seen him in person since I broke it off with him. He carries himself differently. Less happy-go-lucky. More mature. "How did you even know where to find me?"

"Your doorman told me when I explained how important it was that I get in touch with you."

Though I know Jeremy thinks he was doing me a favor by telling Nathan where to find me, I'm going to have to talk to my doorman. Only my aunt is on the need-to-know list. No one else. Sighing, I spread my hands wide. "What's so important it couldn't wait until I got back to town?"

Nathan gives me a cocky smile. "I got your job back."

"What?" My face flushes and I mentally count to ten before I reply so I don't scream at him. "If I'd wanted my old job back, I would've reapplied like everyone else. I told you to leave it alone, Nathan. Why is that so hard for you to get?"

"Because you didn't deserve what happened to you. And yes, I'm not going to lie, I can't accept that there isn't an *us* anymore, Talia." He takes my hand and locks his fingers with mine. "I want you to let me love you, *really* love you."

I pull my hand free. "If you really care about me like you say you do, you would've listened when I told you that I didn't want my old job back. Certainly not like this…with you going around behind my back asking for favors."

His eyes widen. "I didn't ask for favors. I just talked to a couple of people. They're impressed with your success as a mystery author. They said it would be a great way to bring you back, using the book angle as a jumping off point for your return."

"Why didn't they come to me, then?"

"Once I pointed out to them what a great asset you can be, the contacts you've made with all your research, believe me, Talia, they're all on board. Henry was worried you wouldn't take this job offer if it came from him, so he asked me to extend the offer to you on his behalf. The catch is, they have to fill the open slot by next Friday. They want you, but they'll need to know if you're coming back by Thursday. That's why I'm here."

Of course my old boss would think I would refuse any job offer coming from him. He's the one who gave me the hardest time. "Henry was right not to call me. I will never work for that asshat again."

Disappointment flickers, then Nathan's brown eyes light up. "What about Stan? Would you work for him? He's been promoted and is Henry's peer now. He was also the biggest supporter of you coming back, but because Henry knew you first, he let Henry make the offer."

I like Stan. He was always a straight shooter. I chew my bottom lip, wondering if I can balance the demands of working for the paper while writing on the side. I might actually be able to swing it. "Tell Stan I'll come see him on

Wednesday." When a huge smile spreads across Nathan's face, I hold my hand up. "I appreciate you helping me out, but I want to be very clear that if I come back, you and I are just colleagues."

He nods. "I know I screwed up. I'll just be happy to see your face around the office again. You were truly missed. I can't tell you how much."

I shake my head. "I'm not agreeing to anything, yet. I'm just going to talk to Stan."

"Understood." Nathan runs a hand through his hair. "I'm not going to lie, Talia. Seeing that guy go down on you—" He pauses and exhales a shaky breath. "Damn, that was hard as hell."

I arch my eyebrow. "Welcome to my world."

He gives a resigned sigh. "It really does drill the point home rather *painfully*. For what it's worth, I feel the need to say it again. I'm truly sorry that I hurt you. I've regretted it every day since." When I nod, he gestures toward the elevators. "You want to get a drink with me for old times sake?"

"If I take the job, I'm sure there will be a celebratory round of drinks at Cooper's. I'll raise a glass with you and the other staff at the pub then."

"Fair enough," he says, sliding his hands into his black slacks' pockets. "Well, I guess I'd better go check in."

I blink at him. "You're staying?"

He shrugs. "I took the last ferry over, so yeah, I'm here for tonight at least. Might even stay tomorrow. We'll see."

I don't know how I feel about my ex staying in the

same hotel. Talk about awkward, but it's not like I have any say-so in what he does. "Okay, well, please convey the message to Stan for me."

He nods. "Absolutely."

As I start to walk away, he falls into step beside me. "You're heading back to the ballroom, right? I'll walk with you as far as the lobby."

"Um, sure."

Once we reach the lobby and I start to turn off toward the ballroom, he calls after me in a low voice. "You look especially beautiful tonight, Talia. I hope he knows what a lucky bastard he is."

"Thank you, Nathan." *I have no idea what Sebastian thinks.* "Enjoy your evening."

My stomach clenches as I enter the ballroom once more. The crowd has dispersed some, with people moving off to talk in smaller groups or by the cash bar. I scan the room, but when I don't see Sebastian anywhere, nor in the main restaurant's bar, I wonder if he went back to his room. A waiter passes by and offers me a flute of complimentary champagne, but I decline and leave the ballroom.

A few minutes later, I knock lightly on Sebastian's door. When he doesn't answer right away, growing tension knots my stomach. Where did he go? Is this his way of saying, "Screw it?"

I don't even know his number—actually he doesn't have a phone anymore unless he replaced it—so I can't call or text him. And with no pen in my purse, I don't have a way to write him a note. Sliding my invitation under his door, I walk away with a heavy weight pressing on my chest.

I've only taken a few steps when the entire one-sided phone conversation in his car hits me. Mina's pregnant! The realization makes me smile past the ache in my chest, then frown again when the rest of his conversation replays in my mind. He must've been talking to his stepmother, Isabel. What paperwork did he sign? He'd talked about tabloids and his lawyer drawing up papers, then right before he hung up, he said, "Get used to it." What would infuriate his stepmother so much?

Ah… my smile broadens and tears fill my eyes. He took his father's last name, which is why his stepmother was so pissed. She'd hoped her husband's illegitimate child would stay hidden from the public, and in doing so he could keep his part of the massive Blake inheritance. I'm so glad Sebastian stepped out of the shadows. I just wish he would do that with me. I suspect there's far more to his past than I'm aware of. Then again, I have my own dark secrets. It's not really fair of me to expect him to bare his soul if I can't.

Once I reach my room, I take my time undressing, dragging out the entire process. In my heart, I hope Sebastian will stop by, but when another half hour passes, I brush my teeth and wash my face before crawling between the cool sheets.

I don't know how long I lay in the dark, staring at the ceiling. At least an hour. I jump when the air-conditioning kicks on, my nerves on a raw edge. Curling into a tight ball, I force my eyes closed. After last night's lack of sleep, my early-morning crazed swimming, and the very busy day I've had, it's finally catching up, and I can't hold my eyelids open any longer.

I awake with a start in the darkness at the jarring sound of knocking on my door.

"You there?" Sebastian says, knocking again.

Heart racing, I roll over, and just as I start to throw the covers off my legs, both my calf muscles quickly cinch into horrific cramps, the kind that steal your breath. Unable to speak, I moan low in my throat and try to flex my ankles while massaging each muscle, but the cramps are just too intense.

"Let me in," he demands, his tone changing, turning harsher.

Wanting to respond, I push my rebelling legs over the edge of the bed and try to stand to force the cramps out, but the second I attempt to put weight on them, my right ankle gives out completely and I pitch into the nightstand.

Ugh! Breathing in short gasps, tears streaking down my cheeks, I apply pressure on the good ankle and start to hop up and down while mentally telling my right ankle to move in circles and wake the hell up.

"Open the goddamn door, T!" Sebastian growls in a low, barely controlled tone.

I gulp a grunt, but I can't even form words to answer him; the waves of agony screaming through my muscles are just too intense.

After twenty seconds or so I'm finally able to use both legs, and as I begin to run in place, the cramps slowly ease out of my muscles. Exhaling a sigh of relief, I call out to Sebastian, "I'm coming. Give me a sec."

Silence greets me. Great. He's gone.

"That's just perfect!" I snap, flopping back onto my bed in sheer frustration. While I consider having the front desk dial Sebastian's room, my legs start to cramp again.

Argh! Jumping up, I grab my cell phone from my nightstand and text Cynthia while I jog in place. I don't care that it's four a.m.

> Me: *What is the name of that masseuse you recommend? I'm dying here. Will have to go as soon as the spa opens tomorrow!*

Once I take some pain medication, I flop back into the bed and hope like hell no more episodes happen before I can get to that masseuse.

CHAPTER TWELVE

Talia

"*If* you'll step right this way, Miss Lone." Theo turns his nicely tanned, six-foot frame and gestures to the table already lined with fluffy white towels. Soft music, featuring flutes, drums, and the sound of rushing water pumps through the speakers, while a light sandalwood scent floats in the air.

"Thank you for seeing me so quickly. My friend Cynthia recommended you."

He inclines his head, smiling. "Of course. I believe you requested a hot stone massage?" he asks in a Swedish accent, light green eyes assessing me.

I nod. "I've never had a hot stone massage before, but a friend recommended it. I understand you do deep tissue as part of the massage. I'm not sure if deep tissue is what I need. I've just had the worse night of leg cramps ever."

His blond brows pull together slightly. "Is this a common occurrence?"

I shake my head. "Not at all. Apparently, I overdid it with spontaneous exercising yesterday."

Nodding his understanding, he hands me a neatly folded towel. "I'll step out while you remove your clothes."

I clutch the towel between my fingers. "All of them?"

A reassuring smile tilts his lips. "It's up to you. I move small towels around as I work, but it's really best with no other clothes to impede the stone's fluid movements."

After he steps out, I remove all my clothes, tuck my phone and room key inside them, and then lay down on my belly with the towel he gave me draped across my butt. I want these cramps worked out of my legs before I try to find Sebastian. I barely slept the last couple hours before I could call and make an appointment at seven-thirty this morning.

Theo returns a few minutes later, and the moment he begins to move the hot stones across my upper arms using a light aromatic oil to help them glide across my skin, I groan my approval.

He chuckles lightly. "Good, yes?"

"Heavenly," I breathe out and let my entire body relax into his expert hands.

Ten minutes later, once he's moved past my shoulders and arms, he pauses for a second and mutters in his native language.

"Is everything okay?" I ask only because I don't want him to stop. *Ever.* Damn, why haven't I gotten a massage before now? It would help relax my body so much after spending hours in the same position at the computer.

"The power light appears to have gone out on the unit that heats the stones. If you're okay laying here for a few minutes, I'll just run across to our other spa and grab that one, so I can keep going with your massage."

"Sure," I mumble, barely awake, my head resting between my raised arms. I'm so relaxed and sleepy, he could be gone a half hour and I wouldn't move.

I've just closed my eyes when strong hands slide across my back and down my waist. "I guess you couldn't get the unit." I sigh. "I miss the stones, but I'll probably need your hands on my legs more than the stones anyway."

His hands move to my feet and begin to massage them with just the right amount of strength and skill. *God, that feels good. He has amazing hands. I was missing out while he used the stones.*

"This is better." I sigh happily as he moves to my ankles, then my calves, paying special attention to the muscles. "They're crazy tight, right? God, it was embarrassing how many times I had to jump out of bed last night."

Theo's hands still on my calves. A second later he slides his thumbs around, digging deep into the calf muscles. "Ow!" I arch slightly, waving my hand behind me like a white flag. "Okay, I guess I can't handle deep tissue. A bit softer is probably best."

He resumes massaging with less vigor, working his way to the back of my knees. Circling his thumbs in the most sensitive spots, his hands continue to glide up my thighs, kneading and working the muscles until my legs feel completely loose and relaxed.

"Cynthia was right. You have fantastic hands," I say, sighing in blissful pleasure.

In response, he moves his thumbs higher, pressing them along the inside of my thighs. He applies just the right amount of pressure to let me know he wants more room. When I move my legs apart just a bit, he digs in, his fingers working their magic on the back of my legs. I tilt my head slightly when his thumbs continue to move higher and I feel the towel edge up.

God, that really feels good, but I can't help but tense slightly. His hands are a little too close for comfort considering I'm naked under the towel. The second his thumbs brush the crease where the back of my leg meets my butt, I start to jerk myself up onto my forearms. A hand presses between my shoulder blades, pushing me back down before he leans across me and says in a low growl, "What acrobatics were you doing all last night that gave you leg cramps? Because you sure as hell weren't in your room."

Shit! Sebastian. His intoxicating smell only adds to the arousing pressure of his hard chest pinning me to the table. Of course the man gives one hell of a massage. Is there anything he isn't masterful at? "Where's my masseuse?" I demand.

"My guess is he's currently picking out a new car," he says in an annoyed tone as he lifts off my back, but keeps his hand firmly in place. "You didn't answer the question."

He paid the guy off? Only Sebastian would do something so extreme. Even though his low, angry voice sends shivers down my spine, I let the fact that he's pissed at me amp my own anger over his desertion for most of the night. Shrugging, I answer in a nonchalant tone, "It's not like you were around."

I jump when his other hand swiftly moves between my legs to cup my sex in a possessive hold, then I gasp when the towel disappears and teeth clamp briefly on my ass. Digging the tips of his fingers into the bit of hair between my legs, he folds his hand tight around me and leans across my back once more, husking in my ear, "This was mine first. Not his. You gave yourself to *me*."

My heart pounds like crazy. I'm so turned on, but somehow I manage to keep my voice calm. "And yet you didn't stick around, did you?"

Expelling a harsh grunt, he speaks with menace and intensity. "I went for a run. If I hadn't, I would've beat the hell out of him for daring to touch you. Tell me that you didn't spend the night with him." I'm surprised when he plants a tender kiss on my neck and then another on my shoulder, his tone turning vulnerable in its edginess. "Tell me that you want to be with me."

I love that I can still feel the sting of his light nip on my ass. That he wants me enough to leave his mark. His intense, volatile emotions make my hands shake and heart race at a staccato pace. It was so much easier to keep my distance from him when his powerful presence wasn't rushing over me in a heady wave of masculine smells, decadent, knowing hands, and hard muscles pressing against me. Now I have no control. None. Tears slip freely across the bridge of my nose, but I blink and take a deep breath to stop the flow. I need to maintain some of my dignity with Sebastian, because he's the only man who has the power to completely and totally devastate me.

"I only want to be with you, Sebastian."

As soon as I answer, he straightens, his big hand landing on my rear end with a resounding smack. Sliding his thumb along my tingling butt cheek in a tender caress, he commands in a low tone, "Sauna, five minutes. Don't be late."

The sauna is outside the spa area, so I take a shower to get the oil off my skin before I head in that direction carrying my clothes and wearing a resort robe and flip-flops. I see Donald and another Hawthorne employee along the way. Noting the direction I'm headed, the sandy-haired guy takes a towel off the stack of supplies he's carrying, along with a fresh bottle of water and hands them to me. "You'll need water if you're going to the sauna."

Thanking him, I take the towel and water and make my way down the hall.

I arrive five minutes late on purpose, my stomach fluttering in anticipation. Sebastian needs to know I won't follow every order he gives. Still I'm a bit nervous as I step into the sauna room after stowing my clothes in a keyed locker outside. And of course, *Mister Black* is nowhere in sight.

Frustrated with Sebastian, but relieved no one else is around, I exhale a sigh and pour some water over the hot stones to get the steam going. I set the water bottle on the wall shelf at one end of the bench, then step out of the knee-length robe and hang it and the towel on the hooks underneath the shelf.

Stretching out on my belly, I rest my arms above my head and close my eyes, letting the steam roll over me.

"I don't know whether to be insulted or pleased that you're comfortable enough to fall asleep while waiting for me," Sebastian says in a seductive tone next to my ear.

Blinking to shake away my drowsiness, I laugh. "Probably a bit of both." Just as I lift my head, intending to sit up, something tugs on my wrists above my head, keeping me locked in place.

I jerk my gaze to the silky gold rope knotted around my wrists, recognizing it from the long drapes that cover the windows across the entire resort. Sebastian tugs on its secured trailing-end tucked somewhere under the end of the bench. Dark eyebrow raised in challenge, he smirks. "See what happens while you sleep? Next time, don't be late."

While he squats in front of me in nothing but a towel wrapped around his washboard abs, his words ripple through me. They might sound like a reprimand, but I see the raw desire in his eyes as his fingers slowly trail over my bound wrists then move up my bare arm.

Despite the heat in the room, chill bumps scatter across my skin. My heart thumps hard against the bench. "You can't always have your way with me, Sebastian. If I choose to be late, I'm late."

His bright blue eyes flash and his mouth quirks slightly as his hand moves across my shoulder, then up my neck. I swallow when he unclips my hair and spreads the red curtain across my entire back before trailing the flat of his hand down my spine to the curve of my rear. Throughout his tender exploration of my skin, he doesn't say a word, and for some reason that's more unnerving than the intense Sebastian I'm used to.

Cupping his hand on my butt, he taps my cheek, commanding softly, "Lift your hips."

My aching breasts dig into the wood as I do as he asks, but he shakes his head until I lift myself high enough. I stop when he smiles and slides a rolled-up towel under my hips. With my rear raised in the air and my arms secured to the bench, I feel incredibly exposed, but I bite my lip and wait to see his next move.

"Do you remember your safe word?"

"Do *you*?" I counter.

"Rainbow," he says in a clipped tone, then grips my inner thigh and tugs slightly. "Spread your legs." My skin tingles at his barest touch. I exhale deeply and slide my knee toward him a bit.

Smoldering heat flashes through his eyes and his jaw

tightens, his voice turning rough. "More."

I'm throbbing so much even the curling steam in the room is turning me on.

As soon as I move my other knee, he's on his feet and straddling the bench between my thighs.

"Hey, that wasn't what I expected," I say, frowning as I start to pull my legs together.

Strong hands land on my thighs and he sits, muscular legs blocking me in, holding my legs in place. "No, T," he says in a gruff tone. "No more hiding. I want to see how wet you are for me."

There's sure as hell no hiding my body's response to him in this position. "I don't like not seeing you," I say, while trying to keep my tone even.

"Later," he mumbles as his hands slide sensually up the inside of my thighs. When he applies pressure and separates my thighs even more, he lets out a ragged moan. "You should see how wet you are. All milky sweetness. Dripping for me to fill you up. Fuck, I want to taste you so bad right now. "

"Then do it," I snap, just as frustrated as he sounds tortured.

Instead he smacks the hell out of my ass. "I waited for you at that damned coffee house," he says harshly. Before I can reply, he slaps the other cheek. "That's for letting me believe you were still engaged."

"You assumed I was still engaged. Since you were being such an ass that first day and continued to be one by judging me, you didn't deserve the truth," I say as he massages both butt cheeks at once. I try to glance over my shoulder, but end up rolling partway on my side so I can glare at him. "Are you going to spank me every time I frustrate you?"

For some reason my question makes him smile. Grasping my hips, he tugs me back over onto my belly. "Lay still and take it."

When I try to tug free of his hold, he moves quickly, sliding his hard, muscular body over mine. As he pins me to the bench, his arousal juts against my ass through his towel. He speaks in a warm honeyed voice next to my ear. "Trust me. I promise you'll come long and hard. Give in and feel."

I'm breathing hard, both angry and turned on, but I finally rein in my initial response and slowly nod.

"That's my girl," he says, nipping at my ear before he slides back to his earlier position.

When he slowly trails his fingers along my back and down my butt, then gently pulls my cheeks apart, I still myself as I wait for the next smack to my rear. "Do you know why I spank you here?" he asks in that sexy deep voice of his right before he delivers another blow in the ultra sensitive skin along my butt crack.

"Because you're a sadist?" I grit out.

He chuckles as he tenderly rubs the flat of his hand against the spot he'd just reddened with his hand. "I'm not going to say you don't deserve a rosy red ass for the number of times you've given me a hard-on the last couple of days."

I stiffen and huff, "That's not my fault," right as he whacks a bit lower down my butt and much closer to my sex.

Pain and desire swirl through me fast and furious, but all I can focus on is the sting. "Watch it. That's a bit too close," I snap, annoyed with myself for letting this turn me on.

He grunts and rubs his thumb along the heated skin. "What happens when you get aroused?"

"What?" I pant, surprised by the question.

"Tell me what physically happens to your body," he demands just as he lands a forceful tap on my other ass cheek. It's so close to my intimate parts, I actually feel a deep jarring sensation, followed by warm tingling throughout my entire center.

"I um…bl—blood rushes south?" I stutter as my body starts to shake with a raging need for release.

"Is that a question or a statement?" he asks, smug amusement lacing his words.

When I can't form a response, he stands at the same time he cups his hand over my sex. Slowly winding his other hand into my hair, he gently tugs my head back. "You don't know?" he asks in a low tone, his voice tighter than it was a second ago.

Everything inside me centers on the intimate press of his hand against me, of what comes next. I'm vulnerable and achy, but all I can do is shake my head, because I can't believe how easily the man can bend my body to his will. He's done this to me in the past, but this time it feels different. More…personal. Never in my life would I have thought a spanking could be so intensely sensual. Does he know he's the only man I'd allow to touch me like this?

"I would never raise a hand to you in anger, T. Always and only for pure pleasure. Spanking you heightens the sensual experience and makes your orgasm much stronger." Bending close, he nips at my shoulder and commands, "Come for me, sweetheart," at the same time he grabs onto my sex with just enough force to send me spiraling over the edge. I shake as my orgasm rushes along my nerve endings. Heart racing, my body clenches in such a visceral response, I grip the rope between my fingers and pant through the experience, while wondering if I might actually pass out.

Once my hips stop moving and I try to catch my breath, he presses a hot kiss to my neck, his own breathing shallow. "I'll never get enough of how responsive you are to my every touch. You're fire burning through the shadows all around me, and it's the hottest turn on, T. So fucking hot."

Standing, Sebastian quickly unhooks the rope, and just when I move to my knees and hold my wrists out for him to untie, he lifts the end of the rope up. I'm too busy staring at his tanned, muscular chest and arms, and the two sexy bands of muscle that dip underneath the towel riding low on his hips to notice that my hands are rising in front of me until he loops the end of the rope onto one of the hooks under the shelf.

"Hey!" I tug on the hook, rattling the water bottle on the shelf above it. "It's time to let me go now."

"I'm not done with you yet." Shooting me a merciless smile, he quickly straddles the bench behind me and runs his hands down my sides. I arch into his hands when he pauses to lightly caress my breasts before he slides his palms to my waist. "Now turn around."

There's enough play in the rope that I can turn without issue, but apparently I don't do it fast enough. Sebastian quickly picks me up as if I weigh nothing and sets me down on a towel.

While we face each other in the warm, steamy room, he raises an eyebrow at my bent knees pressed to my chest and my ankles crossed in front of my private area.

I eye the towel he's still wearing. "One of us needs to lose the towel."

His jaw muscle jumps as he slowly wraps his fingers around my ankles. "I just made you come by spanking you. If you trusted me enough to do that, then baring yourself to me now should be easy."

No, it's harder. I can't hide anything from you this way, and you see too damn much in my eyes. I tug on the rope around my wrists. "It'd be easier if I could touch you."

His mouth tilts in the slightest smile. "Not yet."

"Why not?"

Before I can lock my legs in place, he quickly pulls them apart and places my feet on top of his thighs. "Sebastian!" I hiss.

"Leave them here," he says in a stern tone before

tracing his finger along the inside curve of my left breast. I hold back a gasp of surprise when he cups my breasts in a firm hold and dips his head to slide his nose down the middle of my chest. He inhales deeply against my cleavage, then slowly exhales. Releasing me, he trails a single finger down the center of my body. "Why didn't you see me in Bash?"

His question sounds conversational, but his focus remains on his hand as he slides his fingertip past my stomach to the small patch of red hair between my legs. For a split second, with his nose pressed against me a second ago, Sebastian appeared as vulnerable as I feel whenever I'm with him, so I answer him honestly. "I thought I recognized you in the helicopter, but then you pulled your glasses down and your eyes were different. Are you wearing contacts to change your brown eye while you're being Bash?"

He lifts his gaze to mine as he dips his finger just inside my entrance. "When you pulled off your glasses in the helicopter, I recognized you instantly. And no, I'm not wearing a contact. I got caught in a bomb's blast radius during a mission a couple years ago. Apparently a head injury can change eye color."

"I'm sorry. I didn't know." I remember the scar across his right hand and scan over his face, looking for more damage. That's when I notice the thin red line curving around the side of his throat. "Did that blast affect your voice too?"

When he nods, I blink back tears. I can't let him see

them, because I know he's the type of man who wouldn't want my sympathy, but I can show him. "Release me, Sebastian."

"Not yet," he says, his tone fierce as he slides his finger deep inside me.

My breath catches, and I can't help the moan that slips from my lips. If he's not going to let me comfort him physically, all I have left to offer are my words. "There were other things you said and did as Bash that made me wonder."

He slides two fingers into my channel, then begins to move them in and out of my body in a torturously slow pace. "And yet you wouldn't have dinner with Bash because he reminded you of me." Pushing his fingers deep, he curls them forward and slowly rubs them along a part of me that has never been touched. Whatever he's doing feels so good, I try my best not to physically shake, but I can't stop my eyes from closing in sheer ecstasy.

"Sebastian," I breathe his name. My whole body is arched, a taut bow's string ready to be released as passion builds in me once more.

"You said, 'It was good and bad,'" he grates out.

I mentally wince at his interpretation of my earlier comment. "That's not exactly how I meant it."

"Look at me," he demands while he continues to wind me tighter, spiraling my passion.

"I—I can't," I say, shudders of pleasure quickly building and spreading to every single nerve ending.

He leans over and captures my nipple between his

teeth, applying just enough force that I jump and open my eyes on a gasp.

My quick movement sends the water bottle slamming to the wood floor, but while the bottle's popped lid leaks its entire contents between the thick slats, Sebastian doesn't lose his focus. His blue eyes remain locked with mine, reflecting frustration and heat. Curving his fingers deeper, he applies pressure, taking full advantage of the spot he's found. "How is this anything but *good*?"

Unable to control my response, I give myself over to the heart-stopping orgasm. As my body begins to contract in rapid, forceful pulses of pure bliss, I'm shocked by the gush of warmth that spreads across his fingers. My face instantly flames and my voice shakes in embarrassment. "Oh, God, did I just…?"

He flashes a smile, full of male satisfaction. "No, but you did just give me something very sweet to savor." Jamming his wet fingers into his mouth, he groans and buries his nose between my raised arm and throat, his whole body taut.

Relieved he appears just as caught up, I try to wrap my legs around his hips to pull him closer, but Sebastian grips my thighs and holds me still, his warm breath rushing against my throat. "If you connect with me right now, I'm so primed, I'll either fuck you senseless or explode. Just… give me a minute."

"What's wrong with fucking me senseless?" I ask on a pout.

A pained grunt reverberates against my neck. "Who's

the sadist again?"

While he's resting his head on my shoulder, I whisper in his ear, "With you, there's a fine line between good and bad. Your intensity doesn't scare me, Sebastian. Your tenacity does."

He looks at me, the tension in his body less pronounced but still there. "My tenacity goes hand-in-hand with my instincts. The two have never steered me wrong. When I go after something I want, I don't give up until I succeed."

I'm almost afraid to ask, but I need to know. "And what do you do with acquisitions that turn out not to be as big a prize as you first thought?"

His lips curl upward in a predatory smile. "If I take the time, it was worth the effort in the first place."

I glance away. *You would look at me differently if you knew everything I've done.*

Hooking his finger on my chin, he turns my face back to his. "I'm the one who showed up at the coffee shop. I won't let you chicken out this time." Glancing around the steamy room, he continues, "The last place I want to have sex with you is on this wooden bench. I want you in my own space with lots of time to indulge, but I have morning flight runs to make, starting in less than an hour." He runs his fingers through my hair, pulling the strands forward and over my breasts. "So beautiful," he murmurs before his eyes snap to mine, full of renewed intensity. "Have dinner with me later."

When I nod, he sets his forehead against mine, exhaling deeply. "Be ready at four. Wear something casual. I'll come by your room to get you."

"Four's kind of early for dinner, isn't it?"

He presses a kiss to my forehead. "Not for the plans I have."

Intrigued, I smile and start to kiss him, but he shakes his head. Jaw tensing, he traces his thumb across my bottom lip. "When I kiss this sassy mouth of yours, I'm not going to stop until I'm balls deep and you're coming all over me. Got it?"

Breathless, I hold his gaze and kiss his thumb. When his bright blue eyes shift to turquoise, I slide my lips down his thumb all the way to the base, humming my understanding.

His eyes turn stormy as he folds his other fingers around my jaw. Sliding his thumb under my tongue, he cups my face in a possessive hold and rasps against my ear, "You're going to find out later what happens when you push my buttons."

The primal rawness in his voice sends a shiver racing through me. I release his thumb with a wet smack, then kiss the tip. "So glad to know I have something to look forward to."

He lets out a low chuckle and nips at my ear, just hard enough to make me clench in anticipation. "When you're writhing and begging me to let you come," he says in a sinful tone, "Just remember, you asked for it."

CHAPTER THIRTEEN

Talia

"*Dinner* was superb, and then Dan took me to this dance club over in Chappaquiddick." Cynthia takes the last bite of her lunch croissant, her long eyelashes fluttering in excitement.

"It sounds like you had a great evening," I say, taking a sip of my peach tea.

Her blonde curls bob. "It was a fantastic night. I can't wait to see him later today. What about you? Did you find your perfect match at the ball last night?" Snickering, she waggles her eyebrows. "Do tell. I'm sure those leg cramps didn't come from nothing…"

Just when I start to speak, my phone rings.

Glancing up as I pull my phone out of my purse, I see Nathan across the room waving and pointing to his phone.

"Excuse me for a second, Cynthia. It's business." I quickly put my phone to my ear. "Did you talk to Stan?"

"He's calling me back in ten minutes. Can you end your lunch early and come over here? It looks like the lunch crowd is clearing and we'll have the room to ourselves in time for a conference call with Stan."

"I can talk to him on my own, Nathan."

"Yeah, but I've worked with him longer than you have. I can help. Just let me, okay?"

"All right," I say on a sigh. "Just give me a few minutes."

Nodding, he hangs up.

I smile at Cynthia. "I'm sorry, Cynthia, but I have a meeting I need to attend."

Her mouth purses in a slight pout. "But I thought you were on vacation. You're not supposed to be working."

Her comment makes me smile. "Well, technically this is in relation to another job I'm considering."

Blonde eyebrows shoot up. "Oh, what do you do?"

"I solve mysteries with words."

She laughs. "Ooh, so cryptic."

I snicker. "I'm an author, but this job will be in addition to that. I really need to go to a meeting with an old work colleague who happens to be here this weekend."

"I understand." Sighing, she puts some cash down for her bill, then stands. "At some point I hope you and I can have some fun girl time together like we did when you first got here."

I stand as well and smile. "Definitely."

Nodding, she slides her purse on her shoulder. "Dan and I have plans the rest of the day. Ooh, I know, how about you and I go walking on the beach tomorrow? Maybe watch the sunrise or, depending on how well my evening with Dan goes, the sunset?" she finishes as she backs away, a wide grin on her face.

Laughing at her cheeky smile, I wave her on. "Sounds like a plan."

On my way over to Nathan's table, I overhear three ladies chatting excitedly. My steps falter as a familiar name bleeds through.

"—pilot, Bash?" the thin, mousy-faced woman addresses a blonde and a brunette. I slow my quick pace as she continues talking. "I passed him in the hall on his way out to the helipad. That man was all kinds of sexy before, but have you seen him since he cut his hair and shaved his beard?"

"Bash shaved his beard?" the woman with long black hair asks, then snickers. "I liked him a bit scruffy. That tells me a man doesn't mind getting dirty."

"And he cut his hair?" the other woman chimes in. "This I have to see for myself. Maybe I'll book a flight lesson just so he'll have to strap me in all nice and tight," she says with a high-pitched titter.

"All I know is that man is fine," the first woman says. "And I don't know why, but now his gorgeous eyes appear even bluer."

Setting my jaw, I resume my normal pace and make

my way over to Nathan.

After an hour of back and forth with Stan, Human Resources, and other upper-level management, I finally agree to return to the Tribune, but only after my book is turned in. While they wait for me to return full-time, Stan asks me to do some preliminary background research for a few projects he has in mind. I agree to handle the research while working on my book.

And because the position needs to be filled now—or it'll be axed with the next quarterly budget review—the Tribune is putting me on salary starting next week. For once, bureaucratic red tape works in my favor.

While I finish up the details with Stan, Nathan waits patiently.

As soon as I hang up, Nathan sets a glass of white wine in front of me. Holding his own glass up, he says, "Congratulations and welcome back, Talia."

When I raise my eyebrow, he says, "Come on. This is worth celebrating."

He did just help make it happen. Having a glass of wine with him only seems fair. I pick up my glass and tilt it toward him. "Thank you for talking to Stan for me."

"I'm just happy to have you back," he says, tapping his glass to mine.

It's on the tip of my tongue to remind him that *he* doesn't have me back, but saying anything at this point would be petty, so I let his comment slide and take a sip of my wine.

Twenty minutes later, I enter my room and start to

head for the closet to pick out something nice for my dinner with Sebastian, when I notice my bed is in a weird state of being stripped, with the comforter and top sheet pulled off and at the end of the bed. Shaking my head at my partially made bed, I walk into the bathroom to double check before I dial the front desk.

"How may I help you, Miss Lone?"

"Hi, I can tell that I've had room service, because I have fresh towels, but for some reason the maid started to change the sheets on my bed, yet didn't finish. Would it be possible for her to do it while I'm gone? I'll be out of the room in an hour."

"My apologies, Miss Lone. Yes, we'll be sure to take care of that for you. If you need anything else, don't hesitate to ask."

With that out of the way, I turn to the closet and expel a nervous breath as I slide each piece of clothes across the bar with a critical eye. *I wish Sebastian would've told me where we're going.*

As soon as Sebastian knocks, I quickly slip out of my room and close the door behind me.

He peruses me with a wicked smile, then puts his hand on the door above my head and steps close. "Are you in a hurry, Miss Lone?"

Thankful I'd worn heels so he wouldn't completely tower over me, I take in the open collar of his crisp medium blue dress shirt and slate gray suit, loving that he'd gone without a tie. Even though he's adopted a more casual look, Sebastian's very presence—from his arousing masculine scent, to the charisma he exudes, to his striking blue eyes assessing every inch of me—screams dominance. He's very much the predator measuring his prey's worth before staking his claim.

And I want to be staked so bad I can't stand it.

"My room isn't clean right now," I breathe out. "The maid left my bed in a bigger mess than it was when I got up."

Lifting a curled end to my hair to his nose, he inhales, his eyes turning darker. "Messy can be fun."

I swallow and force myself not to imagine Sebastian's idea of "messy fun." Otherwise I'm sure my face will turn bright red. "I thought you had a timeframe you wanted to keep."

He releases my hair and slides a finger down my throat to the V the emerald green wraparound dress creates between my breasts. "Sexy casual suits you."

I feel my face start to warm and let out a nervous laugh, tapping his unbuttoned collar. "Back at you, but why do I have a feeling yours is just for show?"

Sliding his hand down my body, he slips his fingers behind the matching silk wraparound belt at my waist and yanks me close to whisper in my ear. "Clothes are only trappings that when stripped away reveal the true beast in us all."

As my breathing ramps, he runs his lips along my

cheek until his mouth hovers over mine. "And because nothing about us has *ever* been casual."

His mesmerizing eyes hold me in place, and my stomach clenches as I wait for him to press his mouth to mine and end the torture. Instead, he releases my belt and brushes his knuckles along my cheek, murmuring with a dark chuckle, "And *this* suits you even more."

Just as it occurs to me that he's referring to my flushed cheeks, he slides his hand down my arm and threads his fingers between mine, tugging me along. "Let's go, Miss Lone. Our evening awaits."

I'm surprised when Sebastian turns his car into the small fishing village of Menemsha in Chilmark, population eight-hundred sixty-six.

While Sebastian speaks to a man who looks like a ship's captain in a black-billed white cap at the end of the harbor, I stroll along the dock, checking out the shops, fishing cottages, and boats.

After I watch a couple of lobster boats come in with the day's catch, I lean on the dock's railing and inhale the salty air while soaking in the sun's late afternoon rays. The warmth feels so good on my face and shoulders, I take my sunglasses off, close my eyes and bask.

I jump when something cool slides around my neck and along the front of my breasts. As I glance down at the twenty-four-inch strand of black pearls Sebastian is settling around my neck, he says in my ear, "I've never seen a piece of jewelry fit a woman more perfectly. Would you like me to take off your gold chain?"

Holding the luminous pearls up, I glance at him over my shoulder and shake my head. "No, I never remove it. The pearls are gorgeous. It's a beautiful gift, but it's too much."

He turns me around and cups my chin, his mouth set in a determined slant. I can't see his eyes past the aviators he's wearing, but I sense his sincerity. "It's a gift with no attachment to it whatsoever other than I thought they'd be perfect on you." As I lower the strand, his gaze drifts down the pearls against my fair skin to my breasts. Snapping his attention back to my face, he smiles. "If I'm going to give you a necklace, I want it to be one worthy of you."

"Thank you," I say, a bit choked up at his sentiment. Smiling, I lift up to kiss him on the jaw, but Sebastian's mouth meets mine instead, his lips firm and solid.

Sliding his fingers into my hair, he cups the back of my head and slowly traces his tongue along the seam of my lips. His kiss is so enticing and seductive, my body instantly heats at least ten degrees.

The second his tongue slips past my lips, someone clears his throat behind us. "Excuse me, Mr. Black. Your boat's ready, sir."

The "boat" the ship captain guy is referring to turns out to be a forty-foot yacht parked at the end of the dock. Once Sebastian escorts me aboard, he pulls a chair out for me at a small table not far from the railing on the front deck, then slips off his jacket.

When he starts to roll up his sleeves, I ask, "Are you

going somewhere?"

He flashes a boyish smile. "You don't expect this boat to move itself, do you?"

I open my mouth, but nothing comes out. I'm just so surprised. Tracing his fingers along the back of my neck, he says, "Enjoy the ride. I'll be back in a bit."

Of course I don't stay put. I follow Sebastian and watch him get into the captain's seat and start the engine. For the next twenty minutes, he steers us out of the slip and into the open water, all this done while he discusses so many nautical terms with the ship's captain that I lose count. We don't go too far from shore, but we're out far enough that I'm glad I know how to swim. Finally he cuts the engine and hands off the job to the captain. He pauses on his way down the short flight of steps when he sees me watching. "That's the 'water' part, isn't it?" I say quietly.

With a quick nod, he settles his hand on the base of my spine, and we walk together back to the front of the boat. Once we reach the area where we have complete privacy, I lean against the rail and let the sea breeze kiss my face. "Do you miss being in the Navy?"

Mimicking my stance, he squints at the sunlight hitting him directly in the eyes despite his shades. "I do sometimes."

"What about being a SEAL?"

He glances down into the water. "Once a SEAL, always a SEAL. The mindset doesn't change."

"Why didn't you tell me about your SEAL status that night?"

He looks at me, his mouth hardening. "Why didn't you tell me your name?" Before I can answer, he rolls his stiff shoulders. "A SEAL doesn't go around bragging about it. It's not something we advertise."

Nodding my understanding, I return my gaze back to the horizon, enjoying the sun's golden reflection on the water. I can't imagine the kind of missions he's had to do. "Have you ever killed anyone in the line of duty?"

He gazes back out at the water, his voice is quiet and steady. "I was the sniper on my team."

I stare at his profile. "The first time must've been hard."

"It's never easy to take another man's life, even if he is the enemy. Staying focused on the mission was all I could do."

I turn back to the ocean and several moments of silence fill the air between us.

"Why didn't you tell me your name?"

I feel his penetrating stare on the side of my face, but I keep my own focused on the water. "For the same reason I still haven't. My name doesn't matter."

"It does to me," he says, turning my chin toward him. "It did back then. And it does now."

"How long were you gone on your mission?" I ask.

His mouth tightens. "That's not the answer I was looking for."

"How long?"

"Two years."

"And yet it's been three years since we last saw each

other," I say, intending to leave it at that.

"I didn't have *your name* to find you," he says, frustration edging his comment.

I ignore his dig. "You run a security business where I'm assuming you probably do your fair share of investigating..." I pause and raise my eyebrows. "You learned enough from me that night. You knew I went to Columbia where your sister went to school. And I told you I worked for the school paper. How many students do you think fit my criteria?" When his mouth thins, I answer for him. "Eleven, Sebastian. Eleven women fit the criteria. No, I don't think I would've been hard to find if you'd really wanted to find me when you got back." *And as much as that hurts to finally say out loud, for my own self-preservation, I can't let you in too much, either, Sebastian.*

I lay my hand on his suddenly fisted one resting on the railing. "All that said, I'm willing to meet you halfway. The T is real, by the way."

He uncurls his fist and swiftly locks our fingers together. Folding our hands, he runs his thumb slowly over mine. "Why is it so hard for you to trust?"

I blink back the moisture in my eyes, glad he can't see past my sunglasses. "You have no idea how much trust I've put in you already."

Facing me, he traces his thumb along the back of my hand, then pauses to slowly slide it over the suntan line Nathan's ring left behind. "Guess I must've gotten some sun at the festival," I say lightly as I glance up at him.

"You were engaged to him while you worked at the

Tribune."

He didn't form it as a question, but I take it that way. "Yes, we met at work. I broke up with him almost a year ago."

Sebastian's serious expression shifts to a deep frown. "If you broke up with him that long ago, why have you been wearing that damned ring?"

I sigh. "I only came this weekend for my friend Cass, who ended up ditching me at the last minute for a job. I wore the ring to keep guys at bay. I wasn't here for the singles' stuff. Oh, and speaking of Nathan's ring, when we return to the resort, I'd like it back."

His jaw flexes in annoyance. "Why?"

"So I can give it to him before he leaves."

"He's still at the resort?"

I nod. "After lunch, Nathan helped me get in contact with an old colleague at the Tribune."

Sebastian tenses. "You had lunch with him?"

I shake my head and try to let go of his hand, but he doesn't release mine. "No, I had lunch with Cynthia. He happened to be in the restaurant and called me over so he could help me connect with Stan, who wanted to discuss a new job opportunity at the Tribune over the phone."

"You're going to be working together again?"

His tight voice makes me defensive. "What does that have to do with anything?" When he doesn't reply, I sigh. "I'm a professional, Sebastian. I loved my job at the Tribune. I miss helping people and feeling like I make a difference in their lives. Working in the same office with

Nathan is a small price to pay if I can get that back."

His displeased expression relaxes and he pulls me close, wrapping his arms around me. "That, I do understand," he says quietly, burying his nose in my neck. "What about your writing?"

Why do I get the feeling his understanding comes from something personal. Does it have anything to do with him being a civilian now? Wrapping my arms around his shoulders, I press a kiss to his jaw. "I won't go back full time until I finish my last book. And I'll still continue to write even after I do."

He turns me in his arms, then pulls me back against his chest. "Either way, you'll still be solving mysteries with words."

I glance up at him, a huge grin on my face. "You remember that I said that?"

He looks down at me, his voice softening. "I remember everything, Little Red." Glancing out over the water, he adjusts us slightly. "When I first went to live with my Uncle Jack, that summer he brought Calder and me fishing to this very beach. His wife had passed away a few years before, so family trips for he and Calder became even more important. I remember sitting on the beach and watching father and son interact, how my uncle teased Calder mercilessly. It was on that trip that I realized he treated me the exact same way. That was the best summer and what was equally memorable." He trails off, nodding toward the water. "Watch this…"

I follow his line of sight and gasp at the glorious

sunset.

"It's breathtaking, isn't it?" he says, sounding nostalgic.

I nod, choked up at the beauty and the fact that he wanted to share something so intensely personal with me.

Taking off his glasses, he bends close, his lips tickling my ear. "If you were writing that sunset, how would you describe it? Paint a picture for me."

I take my glasses off too so I can get the colors just right. Resting my arms over his around my waist, I try my best to capture everything I see. "The sun's a ball of fire sitting on the edge of the world, ready to slip into the night. Though its brightness can never really be contained, only hidden from view, the last rays of the day reflect off the water in shades of orange, purple and pink. Sparks of yellow skip along the wave's crests like dancing fireflies. And in the deeper waters, fiery red-orange veins the dark, rolling waves in thick ribbons of molten lava."

When I glance up at him, I'm surprised his eyes are closed. They quickly snap open, the bright blue reflecting pleasure and a peace I've never seen in them before. "You have a gift. Never stop writing. That was perfect." Kissing my neck, he smiles. "Are you ready to eat now?"

As the sun disappears, soft music begins to flow from the boat's speakers. Just when we sit down at the table, a young waiter comes up from below to light the three tea candles between us. Once the table is lit, another waiter arrives with plates of steamed lobster tail over a light bed of roasted herb vegetables and parmesan crusted polenta.

The first waiter returns, serving me a glass of Pinot. Once we have the deck to ourselves, Sebastian raises his glass of mineral water for a toast.

"To this evening, Miss Lone." His voice drops to a deeper, seductive bass. "May it rival our first one."

I release a nervous laugh and tap his glass with mine, then take a sip of my wine. When he puts his glass to his lips, I ask, "You don't drink?"

He shakes his head and sets the glass down. "Drinking muddles the mind. I prefer to be alert and in top form at all times."

Does the man ever let himself truly relax? Maybe he gets that through exercise. "You mentioned that you run," I say after I take a couple bites of the melt-in-your-mouth lobster.

Sebastian nods and cuts a piece of polenta in half. "I usually run very early in the morning. On the island, I bike part and run part but get in about fifteen miles a day."

I gulp the sip of wine I've just taken. "You bike and run that much every day?"

"Unless I have an early morning flight or some other appointment, then yes, I do it every day."

No wonder he's so freaking fit.

I hold my glass up once more. "And one more toast."

Looking intrigued, Sebastian lifts his glass.

I clink my glass to his. "Congratulations on taking your family name. I know what you gave up to do that."

A wry smile curves his lips. "I didn't take the name to piss off my Dad. I took it to honor his brother. Jack had a heart attack three years ago. The attack weakened him, and it was his dying wish that I take his last name and officially become his second son. So I did, right there in the hospital room with Calder by my side."

My eyes mist and I blink back the moisture. Sebastian has lost his mother and the only man he considered a true father. I'm so glad he has Calder and that he's also close to Mina. "I'm sorry to hear about your uncle. I think it's wonderful you honored his wishes."

He chuckles and sets his glass down, turning the stem. "I honestly think my uncle knew exactly what my taking the Blake name would do to my family. Since he had blond hair, he knew I favored his brother and the moment the papers were official, the tabloids would start conjecturing. As much as he loved me as his own, Jack was tired of the lies. He hated that I had to hide who I was." He shrugs. "I didn't really care, but I did care what Jack thought, so yeah, I took his name."

I smile, my respect for him growing. "And now you're going to be an uncle yourself. I'm so happy for Mina. When did she get married?"

"Last year. I'm not sold on the guy she married, but I hope she remains happy or he and I will have a strong heart-to-heart."

Chuckling, I shake my head. "Marriages aren't always smooth sailing. Obviously she loves the guy since she's having his baby."

Sebastian shrugs and wipes his mouth with the cloth napkin, done with his meal. "We'll see." Running his hand along his jaw, he looks at me intently. "Mina was your source for that article you wrote in college, wasn't she?"

I nod. "She and her roommate were blackmailed into being drug dealers by their professor."

His hand clenches in a tight fist. "What happened to the bastard?"

I sigh my frustration and turn my fork over a couple of times. "He committed suicide while in jail awaiting trial, but at least his whole operation got shut down in the process."

"Thank you for protecting Mina's name," he says in a quiet tone.

I nod. "It all worked out in the best way it could've." Finishing my last bite, I tilt my head. "I know you're close with Calder and Mina, but are you with her older brothers?"

Sebastian exhales a harsh breath. "Damien and Gavin are more difficult to read than Mina."

He said it like an annoyed oldest brother would. I wonder if he realizes that fact.

The young waiter returns as I finish my glass of wine. "Would you like another glass, Miss?"

"She'll have a glass of water, Sam. Thank you."

Once Sam fills my water glass and then leaves, I stare at Sebastian. "Actually, I wanted another glass of wine."

He holds my gaze, not at all apologetic. "Alcohol dulls

the senses. The last thing I want are your senses toned down tonight." Rubbing his thumb across his bottom lip, his sensual words capture my full attention. "I prefer you *highly* sensitized, Miss Lone."

His comment makes my insides jump. I'm damn sure another glass of wine wouldn't muffle any sensations he lays on me. The man is like a blowtorch to my senses. I would pretty much have to be knocked out cold before I wouldn't feel him burning through anything standing in his way, including alcohol flowing through my blood.

While I gnaw on my bottom lip, trying to decide if I'm still put out with him, the engine rumbles to life. As the boat slowly begins to turn back toward the shore, Sebastian asks, "Would you like some dessert?"

"I'd rather have a glass of wine," I say in a dry tone.

He releases a dark laugh and stands. "I think I can come up with other ways to give you that euphoric feeling you seem to be craving." Coming around to my side of the table, he lifts my hand and pulls me to my feet. "Dance with me."

It's easy to forget about wine, dessert, or the reason I might've wanted either the moment he steps into my personal space. As much as I don't want to admit he's right about that, I can't deny the attraction between us.

I smile at the song pumping softly through the speakers. Even though it's an older one that I heard when I was a teen, the song *I've Had The Time of My Life* feels so appropriate as Sebastian pulls me against his hard frame and begins to sway us to the music. It reminds me of summer homes and first sexual experiences. Memories I'll always associate with him.

"Are you thinking about us right now, about that night we spent together?" he whispers in my ear as he slowly spins me around.

My breath catches and I look up at him. "How did you know?"

His hand slides to the base of my spine, pulling me even closer until my hips fully align with his. He smiles, that appealing dimple barely showing, but still there nonetheless. "It's the song."

I nod and rest my head against his shoulder, staring out at the ocean we're leaving behind. "Some memories will last a lifetime."

His hand holding mine tightens just a bit. Pressing a kiss to my hair, he says, "Some memories are so unforgettable, they're worth building on. Look at me."

When I lift my head and stare at him in the darkness, his deep voice vibrates against my chest, resonating all the way to my toes. "And there's nothing I want more than to do that with you."

CHAPTER FOURTEEN

Talia

Sebastian hasn't said a word since we danced on the boat. And other than using a guiding hand on my lower back before I settled into his car, he hasn't touched me either. The moment we're alone in Hawthorne's main elevator, he turns to face me, but he doesn't step close. Instead, he slides his hands in his pockets and skims his gaze over me in a slow, deliberate perusal.

It's unnerving and intense, but I refuse to look away. I watch his attention linger on the pearl necklace he gave me before trailing to my cleavage. I exhale slowly when his attention moves up to my throat and jawline, then to my hair before returning to my eyes.

He's so focused, nothing I say is going to bleed through, so I remain perfectly still, accepting his concentrated study.

When his steady regard lowers to my mouth, it's hard not to lick my lips. Somehow I manage, but as the elevator pings for his floor, I can't keep one side of my mouth from turning up in a half-smile.

"What are you thinking, Miss Lone?"

My smile broadens. "That 'Miss Lone' is a little formal at this point, don't you think?"

The elevator door slides open, and as I start to walk out, he puts his hand on the open door, deliberately blocking my exit. "Anytime you're ready to share..."

When I seek his gaze, he surprises me by lowering his hand to his side instead of pushing me for an answer. I take advantage of the reprieve and lead the way to his room.

As soon as we enter, Sebastian turns on the light by the door and steps farther into the darkness to slide his coat off. Now that we're alone, thoughts of our conversation on the boat make my nerves coil tight in my stomach. Have we built our memories up to be more than it was? But then I remember the sauna, and my bones melt just thinking of how he makes me feel. My mind is so jumbled I stay in the glow of light by the door, busying myself by setting my purse on the table.

I jump when Sebastian's hands settle on the table on either side of me, muscular arms and shirtless heat eveloping my shoulders and back. "You're very quiet," he husks in my ear.

I chuckle. "You didn't say a word the entire car trip

back or the elevator ride up, and you're saying I'm quiet?"

Sliding my hair over one shoulder, he presses his mouth to my exposed throat in a slow, deliberate kiss. "Just because I didn't speak doesn't mean my thoughts weren't loud and clear," he says at the same time I feel a tug on the bow at my waist.

When I start to help him remove my belt, he quickly captures my hands and lowers them to my side, his voice a rough rasp. "Keep them here for now."

Heart racing, I exhale to keep my breathing even and leave my hands where he put them as he slowly unwinds the belt from my waist.

"You have no idea the things I want to do to you," he says just before he loosens the tie inside my dress holding the last bit of cloth against my chest.

"I can imagine," I whisper.

Releasing a low, wicked laugh, he peels my dress completely off before pressing his bare chest against my back. "You can try."

I shiver when he moves away, taking his warmth with him. Even though I'm still wearing underwear and heels, I feel completely naked.

My skin prickles when I hear the silky slide of my belt's material moving against itself. "I've had three years to think of all the things I didn't get to do with you," he continues before his lips barely brush against my ear. "Give me your hands."

Pulse thrumming, I raise them up and then bend my elbows, crossing my wrists behind my head.

He kisses my wrist, his voice husky and amused. "Behind your back. Right above those sweet dimples I can't wait to taste."

My breathing jacks and I close my eyes tight, trying not to panic. *You can do this. You can do this. He's not going to hurt you. He'd never hurt you. You know this, damnit. You know he won't.*

"T," he says, his tone turning commanding.

I take a calming breath and lower my hands behind my back.

The silk belt touches my wrists and I breathe through my nose in forced gusts, but when he moves it higher to just past my elbows, my breathing stops completely.

"Then again, I've had three more years to come up with new ways to make you mine all over again," he says as he pulls the belt and ties it so my arms are hitched back and my breasts are thrust forward.

I hear his words and as much as I want to focus only on his voice—on him and how he makes me feel—my mind is stepping back in time, spiraling. No matter what I tell myself, I can't stop the mental free fall that jolts my breathing to an erratic, frantic pace.

"Three years. Can you feel it?" Sebastian says just before he steps close and clasps my hand. The second he wraps my fingers around his erection, it doesn't matter that he's still wearing pants. His hand folding mine around his hard cock sets me off. I can't control the tears streaming down my cheeks.

"Rainbow, rainbow, rainbow," I babble the word over

and over.

"Shit!" Sebastian quickly follows that up by a long stream of other colorful curses as he yanks the binding down past my hands. The second my arms are freed, I'm lifted in his arms so fast I almost wonder if it was all a horrible dream.

Cradling me to his chest, he walks over to his bed and sits down with me in his lap, whispering in my hair. "I'm so sorry."

When I nod as the tears streak down my face, he slides my shoes off and lays us both down. Pulling the covers over us, he won't let me slide away. He hooks a strong arm around my belly and hauls me against his hard chest at the same time he slides a muscular leg between mine. Once he completely folds his massive body around me, his voice is low and concerned in my ear. "A safe word should never have to be used between us. Fucking ever, T."

"It's Talia," I manage to get out. "Talia Murphy." I want to hear him say my real name just once. I've dreamed about it so long. Only, in my perfect dream world, this wasn't how I pictured finally telling him.

He stills behind me for a second, then exhales and presses a tender kiss to my temple, his voice hoarse. "Whatever it is, Talia, you're not leaving this bed until you tell me."

I don't know how long I lay there silently letting the tears fall. His strong arms around me feel so safe and comforting. I think I'm finally crying for the young girl who couldn't let herself show any weakness back then.

Once my eyes dry up, Sebastian unfolds my clenched hand. Sliding his fingers between mine, his warm breath rushes across my neck. "If you have triggers, I need to know. It's the only way we'll be able to work through them."

I take a deep breath and fold our hands to my chest. Closing my eyes, I let myself go back to that day so he can understand.

I'm so focused on my math homework that I don't hear Hayes step through the door connecting our apartments until his hot breath rushes across my neck.

"What are you working on, Talia?"

Amelia's favorite TV show is on in the living room, completely enthralling her. That's why I'm in here. I can't think with the TV blaring, and I have a major test coming up in two days. I don't have time for Hayes' creeper crap. And why did Walt leave the freaking door unlocked again?

Heart racing, I glance to the right, then snap, "I'm trying to concentrate and you're not helping."

Hayes' hand lands on my notebook, covering it completely as he leans over me. "How about you concentrate on me for once."

He smells of smoke and beer. I want to hold my breath, but panic mode overrules. "Walt..." I call out in a warning voice.

Hayes is blocking me in, and at this point with Walt not responding, I'm just done. "I'll study somewhere else," I say in a snotty tone. Slamming my book closed with an annoyed huff, I stand, then push the chair hard under the table.

Before I can pick up my book, Hayes grabs my arm and yanks it behind my back. Hooking his other hand on the crook of my neck, he shoves me over the back of the chair and presses my cheek against the table.

"After today, you're never going to talk to me like that again," he grates in my ear. Releasing my neck, he twists my wrist even more. His tone is hard and angry, his actions the most violent he's ever been toward me.

As soon as I hear him yanking at his belt buckle and then the zipper of his pants coming undone, I call Walt's name again. I don't care about Hayes' earlier threats concerning Walt's future. All I care about is what's happening right here and now.

"Shut up if you don't want the brat wandering in here," Hayes says, his breathing changing to ragged pants.

I'd forgotten about Amelia in my haze of fear. His comment is sobering, and it takes everything inside me not to scream as he grabs my other hand and yanks it behind my back too. When he folds my fingers around his erection, disgust rolls through me. He lets out a deep groan and grinds his hips against my butt.

Bile rises in my throat and I gag. I try to pull my hand free of him, but his fingers are locked around mine, holding his cock in a vise hold. "Don't you dare let go," he warns, as he rolls his hips and moans deeper.

All I can do is lay there as the bastard uses my hand to jerk himself off along the back of my jeans. When he's done, he smacks my ass, then rubs his cum along my jean-covered butt and then down between my legs. Grabbing my crotch, he fists his other hand around my pinned-up bun and yanks hard as he

*leans over to pant in my ear, anticipation in his satisfied tone.
"You're going to be the best fuck. I can't wait to have you."*

Tears streak down my temple when I trail off...my voice hoarse from telling Sebastian about Hayes.

Sebastian's hand curves around my face. Capturing my cheek, he turns me until I roll to face him. Lowering his forehead to mine, he sounds like he's in pain. "How old were you?"

I put my hand on his jaw and feel the muscle twitching under my palm. "Thirteen."

A stillness settles into his hard frame. "This was your neighbor? A grown man who did this to you?" he asks, his voice low and tight.

I nod. "He was Walt's—my aunt's boyfriend—business partner. They cooked and pushed drugs, and dragged me into the business when I was younger."

"I'm going to kill the son-of-a-bitch! I don't give a goddamn how much time has passed!" Sebastian grates out, the bite in his words ruthless and vengeful.

Every part of him vibrates with rage, and this time I press my chest to his and snuggle close, saying in a calm tone, "Hayes is in jail for drug-dealing. He's locked away."

"Not for what he should be," he growls, his voice full of retribution. He clasps my wrist gently despite the anger in his tone. "Where the hell was Walt and your aunt during all this?"

"My aunt never knew and Walt is dead, Sebastian. All the ghosts from my past are only in my head," I finish on a sigh.

He breathes in and out of his nose as if trying to settle his own emotions, then he says quietly, "That's why exposing that drug ring on your campus was so personal to you."

"Yes, and because drugs directly contributed to Amelia's death. She might've been Walt's child by birth, but she was *my* little sister."

Cupping the back of my head, he slides his nose along my throat. "I wish you would've told me."

I snort. "Sure, that's exactly how I'll lead off next time. Want to get kinky with me? Here are a few things that might kill the mood. I'm just sayin'.""

Sebastian expels a pained groan against my throat, then presses a warm kiss there. "I'll understand if you want your space tonight, Talia."

I lean into his kiss and clasp his muscular shoulders tight. "I'll let you in on a little known secret, Mister Black."

His hands move to my back, then glide along my skin to my waist. Aligning my body with his, he kisses my jaw. "Share whatever you want with me, Miss Scarlett Red."

I elevate myself to whisper in his ear. "I only told you because I want to stay. I *want* to be with you."

Before I can settle back into his arms, he clasps my face and slides his thumbs along my cheekbones. "Why did you choose me that night at the party?"

It's too dark to see his face, but the tension in his hold and the timber of his voice conveys unfathomable emotion. "Because you *saw* me."

"I couldn't help *but* see you. Not then and definitely not now," he murmurs against my lips before pressing his mouth to mine.

When Sebastian fully captures my breath, sliding his tongue sensually along mine, each stroke more aggressive than the last, I kiss him back with just as much intensity. Breaking our kiss, his breathing uneven, he reaches for the bedside lamp, turns it on low, then looks at me with serious eyes. "Are there any other triggers? Did anything else traumatic happen to you that I need to know?"

I'm surprised he hasn't brought up that night he drove me home when I was thirteen. He has to know I was way beyond freaked out. I close my eyes and shake my head, shutting it out. I'm glad he seems to want to leave it alone and in the past. Meeting his steady gaze, I keep my voice firm. "Promise me you won't treat me any differently. Things won't work between us if you do."

He slides his hand to the back of my neck and clasps it in a firm hold, arching me even closer. "This is who I am, Talia. The fact that you understand and accept my... intensity, will work to our mutual benefit. I'm not going to lie and tell you I won't worry, but it's not in my nature to hold back. As much as I hate the idea that you might need to use your safe word, it's more important now than ever. I need to know you *will* use it or we may as well end this now."

My heart jerks at the thought that Sebastian would walk away. I don't think I can handle it. Not tonight. Not when my emotions are split open, raw, and on the verge of shattering into billions of tiny sharp-edged pieces inside me. "I'll 'rainbow' the hell out of you if necessary. I prom—" I cut myself off when he lifts the pearls over my head.

Sebastian drops the necklace at the same time he hooks his arm around my waist and quickly slides me onto my back, his voice a low, growling purr. "Don't touch me until I give you permission. Understand?"

My breathing ramps and my insides clench as I watch him snap my underwear off with a deliberate tug on either side. "Do you have to rip them every time?"

His mouth curls in a dark smile as he sits up to push my thighs apart with deft hands. "I've been waiting for dessert all night. Why the hell would I take my sweet time peeling the wrapping off?"

"Anticipation is part of the—" I let out a deep moan when he slides two fingers into my moist channel at once.

Withdrawing his hand from my body, he lifts an eyebrow. "You're soaked already. What were you saying about anticipation?"

I grip the sheets beside me, hating the feeling of emptiness that quickly consumes my body the second he pulls away. Setting my foot high along his thigh, I dig my toes into its thick muscle and slowly roll my hips. "Just that it goes both ways. I know you want to taste me as much as I want you to. Is your mouth watering?"

Smirking, he presses his thumb over my clit at the same time he eases his fingers inside once more. "How bad do you want me to devour you?" he says in a suggestive tone just before he leans forward to capture a nipple between his teeth.

His movement pushes my foot off his leg, but I just dig my heel into the bed instead, curving my body into his hand. I absorb every sensation, enjoying how he works his hot mouth against my breast, tugging with just enough force to make me quiver all over while he strokes deep inside me.

As he trails his mouth along my belly, nipping his way down my skin, I taunt him, even though my whole body is flushed with heat. "I think you want it more."

Sebastian's hands suddenly still my hips' movements. With his dark head bent over me, I feel the rushing heat of his shallow breathing stirring the bit of hair between my legs. I shiver and don't fight against his hands pinning me to his bed.

"I don't *want* it more," he says in a low, tortured tone.

His words are so at odds with the tightness in his shoulders and the near-bruising hold he has on my body, I blink in surprise. I don't get a chance to respond as he spears his tongue through the patch of hair, then straight down my sex in a deeply, possessive thrust, his voice a low rumble, "I'm way beyond wanting, Talia. I've fucking craved your taste for three years."

Fierce need yanks at my belly as he slides his hands along my thighs and lifts me up like I weigh nothing, his hot mouth hovering over me. "But first you're going to tell me why you didn't let your fiancé do this to you."

Is he serious? He hasn't looked up at me, but he hasn't

moved his mouth closer either. Raging yearning tears through me as I swallow. "Why does that matter?" His grip tightens on my ass. "It matters. Tell me." His tone is harsher, more intense. My fingers tighten on the sheets. "I don't know. It...just felt—" "Wrong," he clips out. Not a question, but a statement. My heart lurches. "Why would you say—" "Because I own this," he says fiercely, tension creeping into his body. "You're going to be sore as hell tomorrow, and I won't feel an ounce of guilt. Tonight I'll remind you why this gorgeous pussy is mine and no one else's."

I cry out in amazed bliss when he thrusts his tongue deep inside me, then curls it inward, tracing every fold. Swallowing, he mumbles, "Fuck, you're even sweeter than I remember."

He quickly finds my clit and sucks on the sensitive bit of skin at the same time he presses two fingers inside, going deeper than before. I writhe and rock my hips, whimpering and enjoying his thorough manipulation of my body.

When I press closer to him, Sebastian lets out an inhuman growl of satisfaction at the same time his brilliant blue eyes snap to mine, full of primal ownership. The "mine" in his gaze, the unadulterated possession makes my insides burn thirty degrees hotter. Arching against him hadn't been conscious. With Sebastian, I have no control. I'm lost in the haze of pleasure he's giving me. All I can do is move with his tongue and lips pulling on my skin, making my body quiver with desperate need.

Just when I start to quake, ready for release, he eases the pressure, but doesn't stop arousing me. He builds up his aggressive, body-shaking attention all over again until I'm incoherently rambling, "Please, Sebastian, just let me come."

"Say it."

"Say wh—what?" I pant out.

He sucks on my clit harder, driving me so crazy I close my eyes and moan through the intense experience. Then he hits that spot inside me that makes my whole body bow with raging desire. "Who owns it, Talia?"

Despite my sharply rising need for release, I can't help but feel that if I say he owns my body that means he owns me. No one owns me.

I stop rocking my hips when I feel something cool slide along my wet slit. Once, twice, then a third time. Lifting his head, Sebastian presses his thumb on my clit and his brilliant blue eyes take on a carnal glint. "Do you trust me?"

"You're the only man I've let touch me the way you do," I say even as nervousness curls in my belly. That's as close as I'm going to get to admitting he owns me, more than he'll ever know.

Lifting his thumb, he slides my pearl necklace under it, then lowers his thumb over a bead. Pressing the bead against my clit, he curls his fingers inside me, touching that one place that nearly does me in. "Tell me, Talia. I need to hear you say it."

As I stare at him, he slides the pearl necklace one bead

over and then another. My thighs start shaking and I can't feel my hands I'm gripping the sheet so tight. "Keep me, Sebastian…" I moan out.

His smile turns almost feral. "Come for me," he demands at the same time he gives the wet strand under his thumb a quick tug. The vibrating sensation and sheer eroticism of how he masterfully plays me sends me so far over, I scream and tremble uncontrollably. One orgasm after another races through my body in a crashing blitz of sinfully decadent contractions thrumming through me.

After the third orgasm, I grab his hand to stop the pearls' movement, panting out, "Owned, holy shit! So owned—"

Sebastian's lips cut my words off, his tongue thrusting deep into my mouth. Just when I clasp his neck to pull him fully on top of me, he breaks our kiss and stands to slide out of his pants.

My heart pounds against my chest as he sits down on the edge of the bed with the condom he's pulled from his pants' pocket.

It doesn't seem fair that he shouldn't experience some of what I just felt, and before I give it a second thought, I scoop up my necklace and rise on my knees. Leaning over his hard, muscular back, I kiss his throat as I lower the strand over his hard erection. "It seems only right to return the favor."

When Sebastian exhales harshly, his back muscles tensing against my chest, I take the condom from his fingers and set it on the nightstand. Winding the beads around his cock several times, I circle my fingers fully around the strands and roll the pearls up his erection and then back down, whispering in his ear, "Help me forget."

His breathing amps with my movements. "Are you sure?" His voice is hoarse as he trails his fingers along my wrist.

I slide my body around his until one leg is behind his back and my other is dangling between his hard thighs. Looking up into his hooded gaze, I give him a trembling smile. "Show me what you like."

Sebastian cups the back of my neck, his thumb sliding along the column of my throat. Just as he pulls me into him for a kiss, his hand covers mine around his cock.

"Easy," he says against my mouth, then traces my lips with his. I'm so drawn in by his distracting 'almost kiss' that the sensation of his fingers around mine don't freak me out. I let him set the pace and tightness as he moves my hand along his erection. Clamping my leg around his lower back, I enjoy the feeling of power that rushes through me when his tongue finally slides against mine in a hot, searing kiss.

"Keep doing that," he groans against my mouth as he releases my hand to clasp my face for a harder, even more arousing kiss.

Every part of me centers on Sebastian's masculine scent and heat, the feel of my body wrapped around his hard one. I slow the pace of my hand and then speed it up, listening to his breathing to tell me what turns him on. Every harsh breath he expels into our kiss hikes my own arousal, making me wetter by the second.

Suddenly Sebastian presses his forehead to mine, his words barely coherent. "You need to stop."

I pause for a second, but then I can't help but move my hand up and then back down just one more time.

A low growl erupts from his mouth, and before I can blink I'm on my back and he's above me, the necklace gone as his hard body pins me to the bed.

With his cock teasing my sex and his hands holding mine over my head, Sebastian's breath saws in and out. "What the fuck, Talia? You can't push me like this."

I lift my hips up and slide him just inside my entrance. "And now I know what you like," I say, my own breathing coming in short bursts of air.

"*This* is what I want," Sebastian grates out, surging deep inside me.

I scream with the stinging sensation of my body stretching to accept his impressive size, and I'm shocked to feel my walls already contracting around him in another orgasm.

Sebastian's a hard rock, holding himself perfectly still as my orgasm rips through me. "God, you feel like heaven. My heaven," he says right before he pulls out and then slams into me.

He's so powerful, all I can do is hold on, and when he finally releases my hands, I dig my nails into his back and roll my hips, meeting each of his thrusts with my own.

Just when I feel the euphoric tightness building in my sex once more, Sebastian clasps my hair, his sexy-rough voice a hot rush in my ear as he angles his next hip movement just right, sending me over the edge. Once my orgasm slows, he stops moving, his weight holding me locked in place. "Feel me keeping you, Talia," he says in a tight, guttural groan. As Sebastian comes long and hard, his thick cock pulsing warmth deep inside me, I grip onto his sculpted shoulders and back, feeling taken, owned, and thoroughly enthralled by his savage primalness.

We don't move for several minutes, our heavy breathing the only sound in the room. Still buried inside me, Sebastian lifts his head, stunned disbelief in his eyes. "What are you doing to me?"

I trace a finger along his jaw. "I imagine the same thing you do to me."

He shakes his head. "I always wear a condom."

I smooth his furrowed brow. "Don't worry. I'm on the pill. Everything is fine."

The relief that flashes across his face stabs me briefly in the gut. I don't like that it bothers me. I start to slide out from underneath him, but he puts his hands on either side of me, locking me in place. "Where are you going?"

"To the bathroom."

He frowns. "Do you have to go?"

I shake my head. "I should clean up."

A ravenous smile tilts his lips "You're staying right here." He moves his hips and I'm surprised he's swelling to full hardness inside me already. When my eyes widen, he releases a low arrogant chuckle, then kisses me, his tongue slipping past my lips to tangle with mine. "Three years is a hell of a long time to want," he rumbles against my mouth. "You're not going anywhere."

Sebastian leaning around my shoulder to push a button on his watch wakes me. He'd left it turned on its side on the nightstand, and the backlight is still lit while he settles back into place behind me. My focus stays locked on the watch until the light goes out. One-eleven. Wasn't that the same time his watch had been set to light up three years ago too?

Kissing my shoulder, Sebastian slides out of bed to use the bathroom. As soon as he closes the door, I pick up the watch and push a couple of buttons. He's set it to go off everyday at the exact same time, one-eleven a.m. Why?

When the toilet flushes, I quickly push the buttons to put it back in the mode it was in before and then set the watch back down on his nightstand. He slips back into bed behind me thirty seconds later and hooks his arm around my waist. Hauling me close to his hard body, he runs his nose along my throat and into my hair, his voice a sexy vibration against my back. "I know you're awake."

I roll in his arms and face him, my hand sliding along his hard chest. "Your watch went off at that same time three years ago. What is the significance of one-eleven?"

He doesn't say anything for a second or two, then pulls me close and kisses my forehead. Setting his chin on top of my head, he says in a quiet tone, "It's a reminder."

He cups the back of my head as he speaks, pressing me close, and I can't help but inhale along his skin. I love the combination of deodorant and pure masculine musk. "A reminder of what?" I mumble into his chest.

His arms tighten around me. "To be diligent. Aware. Ready."

I wrap my arm around his body and run my hand up his back. "Ready for what?"

He exhales. "Just…ready."

He doesn't say anything more. I start to press a kiss to his chest, when I suddenly realize that the back of his watch felt smooth against my fingers. What happened to the inscription on it? I pull back and look up at him, my heart racing with concern. "When did you get that watch?"

He stares down at me. "Last week. My uncle had set it up so that as soon as I filed the legal paperwork to change my name, his lawyer gave me the watch." Expelling a laugh, he smiles fondly. "Even three years after his death, Jack continues to make me feel like a part of his family."

I blink up at him, shock rolling through me. "Was the watch a family tradition?"

He shakes his head slowly, bitterness creeping into his tone. "Not really. The watch was my uncle's way of replacing the one I'd lost."

"Oh, I see," I say as calmly as I can. *Damn it! Sebastian never received the watch I left for him? What happened? Why didn't his sister give him the box? And if he never got the watch, that means he still doesn't know I'm Red.* No wonder he didn't ask me about that night eleven years ago. He still doesn't freaking know. As relief and worry battle for dominance in my brain, I bite my lip. Most likely Sebastian never saw what the watch said on the back since he gave it to me the same night he got it.

"I remember you saying your dad got mad when you lost your watch. Have you ever considered the possibility that he gave you that gift because he was proud of you, and not just because it was your birthday?"

His mouth tightens briefly. "He gave it to me as a display of his wealth. Nothing more. Trust me."

"But—" Sebastian captures my mouth in a devastating kiss, cutting me off. "I don't want to talk about watches or asshole parents. Right now I just want more of you, Miss Scarlett Red."

CHAPTER FIFTEEN

Talia

"*What* are you doing?"

I jump at the sound of Sebastian's deep voice overriding the morning news he just turned on in the other room and almost drop the pearl necklace. I lift the strand and gesture to the sink filling with cold water. "Cleaning these. I hope we didn't ruin them."

Leaning against the doorjamb in nothing but a pair of black lounge pants, he frowns and unfolds his arms, defined abs flexing as he steps into the bathroom to turn the water off. "Leave them."

When I glance up at him and start to ask why, he tucks a wet strand of my hair behind my ear. "They represent us, Talia. Naturally raw and beautifully dirty. I don't want to erase that."

As he turns me around, I set the necklace on the counter and giggle to cover how deeply his comment hits me in the gut. "I'd like to wear them again."

"Then I'll buy you another set," he says in a gruff rumble just before he grasps my waist and sets me on the counter in front of him. Stepping between my legs, he slides his hands up my thighs, his gaze following their movement. "Next shower, you're all mine. Got it?"

As his gorgeous blue eyes snap to my face, full of heated desire, I trail my hands up his muscular arms and shoulders. Hooking my fingers around his neck, I tease, "Next time don't sleep in and you won't miss out."

He tugs on the collar of the blue dress shirt I'm wearing, a dark, dominant smile curving his sexy mouth. "Seeing you in my shirt almost makes up for it." He lowers his lips to mine, his voice a husky rasp of sheer sexiness. "I think my clothes should be a required uniform from now on."

I smile against his mouth. "And here I thought you preferred my birthday suit."

He grips the top of my thighs, tracing his thumbs slowly down the damp bit of hair between my legs. "I'll always prefer you wearing *me*, Talia." He smiles, his magnetic charisma pulling me in. I tangle my fingers in his dark hair as he moves closer until his mouth barely touches mine. "On you. In you. Branding you *mine*. Nothing else compares."

Sebastian thrusts his tongue deep into my mouth at the same time he groans and steps into me, pressing his erection against my body. I kiss him back, loving how his possessiveness makes me feel cherished and wanted.

When a knock sounds at the door, he sighs and kisses my forehead. "That's room service. Hold that thought."

I'm surprised when I hear him shut the main door behind him. Curious, I walk into the empty room and notice the TV's sound seems louder. The investigator in me pushes my feet over to the door.

"—thought I'd deliver it in person," a woman's voice floats through the thin wood.

"You didn't have to," he says.

"Aren't you going to invite me in, Sebastian?"

"Now's not a good time, Regan."

A quick feminine laugh sounds, full of smugness. "Really? I thought you were always up for a good time. If your quasi-cousin, or should I say *your h*alf-sister—yes, the rumors are flying all over the local news now—had any idea how kinky you are, I wonder if she'd put you on such a high pedestal."

"You enjoyed every second of it," he says curtly, his tone turning cool.

"Once I got used to you, yeah. Couldn't sit for a week after you left though." Her voice moves closer, dropping to a sexy purr. "I've never forgotten you. I still have that riding crop and collar you bought me. Just looking at them makes me wet."

"I don't do relationships, Regan."

"What was that month then, hmmm?"

"You, coming back for more."

She lets out an annoyed huff. "And here I thought the cocky bastard role was just an act. In light of recent news, you fit it to a T."

"Is that why you're really here? I'll let you in on a little something the tabloids don't know. The moment I took my family name, I lost any claim to the Blake billions."

"That's a shame…" she pouts, disappointment coming through loud and clear. "But regardless of your financial status, it doesn't change how I feel about you. That tells me we had something."

"I was making up for two years of celibacy, Regan. Don't make it more than it was."

"Fine," she snaps, then her tone softens. "For you, I'm willing to let it be just that."

"I'm not interested in renewing our arrangement," he says in a final tone.

Arrangement? I tune out Regan's response. He sounds so disconnected in his responses, I can't help the knot starting in my stomach. *Will that be me one day, begging him to keep me?* Nausea roils in my stomach.

As soon as the doorknob starts to turn, I bolt away, quickly returning to the bathroom. Shutting the door quietly behind me, I blink away the unshed tears and try to shrug off the suffocating ache in my chest. My gaze lands on the necklace, and I push the beads off the counter and into the basin of cold water. *It represents us, my ass!*

Even though I know it's unfair of me to think he wouldn't have had other relationships the past three years, I can't help but feel sick to my stomach that I read so much more into his bullshit lines about us. Should I count myself lucky that a pearl necklace is a step up from a riding crop and a collar? When Sebastian calls my name on the other side of the door, I swish the necklace around in the water and say in a light tone, "Be out in a minute," at the same time I lean over and flush the toilet.

Pulling the sink's plunger to drain the water, I lay the necklace on a hand towel to dry before I walk out of the bathroom. "That wasn't room service?" I glance around, eyebrows raised, my face perfectly composed.

He lifts the shoebox-sized package in his hand. "Just a package from my sister. Room service should be here soon."

"Actually, I thought I'd head back to my room."

Sebastian frowns and starts toward me when the phone on the desk rings. Setting the box down, he grabs the handset, suddenly all business. "Bash."

His dark eyebrows pull down briefly. "Yeah, my new cell phone should be here today. Thanks for the info, Simon. I'll be sure to convey it. There's no need for that. Miss Lone is fine."

"What?" I mouth, but he holds his hand up.

"She's here with me," he continues, his blue eyes holding mine. "Yes, all night. I'll call you later."

My face is flaming hot by the time he hangs up. "What the hell, Sebastian? Why'd you tell the head of security where I was last night?"

He scowls as he moves to tower over me. "Why is spending the night with me so embarrassing to you?"

I stiffen. "I just don't want to advertise my sex life to the whole world."

Sebastian cups the back of my neck, his expression shifting to a less intense one. "Simon is the only one who knows why I'm really here. I told him to keep me informed of any out-of-the-norm activity in relation to you. The fact that someone has been in your room definitely qualifies."

My eyes widen. "Did someone break into my room last night? Wait, and *why* are you really here?"

He shakes his head. "No, the day before. The maid insists she made your bed yesterday, Talia."

I blink at him. "But nothing else in my room was touched. I have a laptop out on the desk. Is it possible she's covering her own hide so she doesn't get fired?"

His mouth thins in a stubborn line as he clasps my hand. "Maybe it's nothing, but in answer as to why I'm here, I'd like you to help me with something." Leading me over to the table, he pulls a chair out. "Have a seat."

I'm not sure where he's going with this, but I do as he asks while he opens his briefcase and sets a stack of labeled beige folders in front of me.

"A couple months ago, I was hired to help the NYPD with their investigation into a string of serial killings. Five redheaded females in and around the New York area have been killed over the course of three years. The murders stopped for two years, then started back up ten months ago when two more women were killed five months apart."

My heart pounds double-time at the disturbing

news, but I try to remain calm. "Other than the fact I'm a redhead, what does this have to do with me? We're in Massachusetts, not New York."

He points to the folders in front of me. "When the serial killer's trail went cold, I did some investigating on my own. One thing the latest two victims had in common was that they'd spent time here at Hawthorne. So I asked Trevor to do some work for my business, while I took his place here to investigate employees who might fit the killer's profile. Nothing told me for sure that the killer worked here. It was just a gut instinct. A lead I wanted to run down."

"For two months?" I ask as I quickly flip open each of the folders to see nine headshots of Hawthorne's male employees: Two tennis instructors, three bartenders, a valet, a waiter, a masseuse, and a personal trainer. Each suspect's picture is paper-clipped to an extensive three-page background check. The extra page of handwritten notes has to be Sebastian's. "That's a long investigation."

"It's a thorough one. I planned to continue until I found the bastard, or if another murder happened elsewhere which would clear the suspects I'd come up with here."

"That's why you didn't want me going anywhere without you," I mutter as I skim the folders.

He runs his finger down my cheek, then hooks it under my chin, turning my face toward him. "Not the only reason, Talia."

I tell myself the warm look in his eyes doesn't mean anything, but I can't help the flutter in my stomach. "Why didn't you tell me about this before?"

"I didn't mention it because I was beginning to believe I'd been wrong in my assumption that the serial killer might work here." Releasing me, he drops his gaze to the folders. "Even though these men fit the basic profile of a single white male who lived in New York in the past, who currently lives alone and is between the ages of twenty-two to thirty-five, none of these employees raised any of the typical red flags I've come across in serial murder cases. Since I arrived, a couple of redheads have stayed here with no life-threatening situations happening to them. And, other than someone drugging your drink at an establishment away from Hawthorne where stuff like that can happen, there've been no other threats against you. That just left you and me, Talia. I didn't want anything screwing that up. Not this time around."

I furrow my brow. "Then why are you showing me these folders now?"

"Because I don't believe in coincidences. The fact that a redhead bought a voucher for a man who ended up killed in a car accident—"

"Mr. Sheehan died?" I ask as my stomach bottoms out.

He nods. "Simon's police contact came through. I had Simon contact him after I learned that Sheehan's rental car went off a bridge a couple miles from here. Even though there weren't any tire marks indicating he never hit his brakes, the police had been at a standstill with his case. They couldn't trace the days leading up to his death back to the resort, since his stay here didn't show up on his credit card.

"But with Sheehan's death and that of your other fan earlier this year, that's four deaths that tie back to Hawthorne; two supposed accidents and two murders involving redheads."

"Don't forget the unknown redhead who purchased the hotel voucher," I remind him.

He nods. "Exactly. Our two cases might not be related, but we can't ignore how their paths cross. You have an investigative mind, Talia. Maybe a fresh set of eyes will see something I missed in these folders. My skills are more tactical and in-the-moment. While everything is in chaos or perfectly still, I see things others don't." He gestures to the paperwork. "After a while, this kind of stuff all blurs together. Would you be willing to look it over while I'm in the shower?"

Combing through this paperwork will be a welcome distraction to keep me from obsessing about the kinky things he did with Mina's friend. "I don't know how much help I'll be, but I can try."

Nodding his thanks, Sebastian heads into the bathroom. A few seconds later, he walks out holding the damp pearl necklace, his voice curt. "Why did you wash it?"

"Sometimes a clean slate is best," I say, holding his intense stare.

Understanding dawns in his expression and he curls his fingers around the necklace. "You heard, didn't you?"

I shrug and look back down at the paperwork.

"I'm not the only one still holding my cards close," he says softly.

Now's a good time to tell him about the watch, Talia. Tell him why you kept it and why you gave it back. I lift my head, intending to speak, but he's already shutting the door to the bathroom. I sigh and whisper, "I'll tell you when you get out."

I flip through each of the beige folders quickly once. The second go round, I put them in order of things that stuck out at me before I settle down to read over each man's background in more detail. When I fill the hotel sticky notes with at least two questions per suspect, I end up with three employees I want to follow up on. As I stare at my notes, I realize that a sheet of lined paper would be best to help organize my thoughts.

Standing, I rifle through more surveillance pictures in Sebastian's briefcase, seeking a legal-sized notepad. When I don't find what I'm looking for, I move to the folder slot section in the top of the briefcase and pull everything out, expecting to find a pad of paper in the stack. He had to have taken those notes on something similar. Instead of paper, I find two more folders.

The first one is blue and labeled Jocelyn Quinn. *Is this Sebastian's mother? You can't read it, Talia. He didn't give it to you.* After I answer the door for room service, curiosity gets the best of me. I open the blue folder, hoping to see a picture and discover if Sebastian favors his mother or his father more. But my heart jumps in my throat and I flop down into the seat, unprepared for the bloody crime scene pictures. I quickly scan through the supporting police notes and paperwork. The investigating police officer suspected a robbery attempt gone bad, but the seventeen-year-old son, Sebastian Quinn, insisted his mother was murdered. Suspects were interviewed but no one was arrested. His mother was murdered? Why?

I run my fingers over the "cold case" stamp on the back of the folder, my heart aching for Sebastian. What a horrible way to lose his mother. I'd always assumed she died of an illness. I start to set the folder down, then a hunch has me opening the folder back up, and I skim through the police officer's notes once more.

> *Son reports his mother woke him a little after one a.m., telling him to get a phone from her nightstand. An intruder was trying to break in. Once he reached his mother, the intruder had broken the lock on the door and shot at Miss Quinn eight times. The mother fell on her son, her body shielding him from the bullets.*

A little after one a.m.? One-eleven. Sebastian had said he set his watch's alarm is a reminder to be diligent, aware, and ready.

Why does he have his mother's file? Is he investigating her death? It makes sense that he would do so now that he has the skills and the connections to dig deeper than the original investigators.

I open the beige folder, interested to see Sebastian's

notes on his mother's cold case so far.

The last thing I expect to see is a picture of me, taken a little over a year ago, paper clipped to the inside of the folder. My hair is still blonde and I'm holding Nathan's hand and glancing up at him as we walk into a restaurant for a dinner party.

Sebastian lied! Why did he pretend not to know my name, when it's clearly plastered all over the first couple of pages of this surveillance report? Why did he push me to tell him? My stomach knots with panic as I flip past the several photos taken during that same year to the detailed handwritten notes about my life. How far back did the guy go? I can tell it's not Sebastian's handwriting. The writing inside the Hawthorne employees' folders is in bold, crisp print. Maybe it was someone in Sebastian's security firm?

Sweat dampens my hands as I scan through the three pages of notes about my life as a college student, the fact that I worked for the school paper, my final grades and College Honors status. Then the notes move on to my rising career at the Tribune. I sit back, relieved to see that the investigator's notes only go back as far as my last year in college.

Yes, I planned to tell Sebastian how our paths had crossed when we were teens as soon as he got out of the shower, but that's it. This folder is the whole reason I never gave him my name three years ago. I didn't want him to find out the truth. If I tell him about our past now, I can't help but wonder if he'd let me leave it at that or if he would push to know what happened that night.

As worry rises up, I take a deep, calming breath. Expelling my breath slowly, I stare at the surveillance notes, baffled as to why the person stopped keeping track of me before I ever left the Tribune. The whole last year-and-a-half of my life: me leaving the Tribune, becoming an author and releasing two books, and my break up with Nathan, none of it is chronicled in this folder at all.

Not that any of this makes sense. Why would Sebastian let me ream him about not looking for me when he'd clearly had *someone* watching me, at least for a little while?

Trying to make sense of him checking into the last few years of my life, I flip through the pictures once more and run across a duplicate of the photo that's paper-clipped to the folder. Only, it's a close up shot of me smiling at Nathan as I hold his hand. Why is this one picture blown up?

Once I reach the back of the folder, I notice a new piece of paper has been added with a one-line note written in Sebastian's handwriting: *Phone tracking activated, Access Code - 542859.* The activation date was the day he saved me outside that bar, which was the only time he had unlimited access to my phone.

As my temper begins to flare, my phone beeps, letting me know I have a text. I glance at my purse on the table by the door. *I can't believe he freaking bugged my phone.* Standing, I quickly walk over to pull my phone from my purse while my mind continues to race. But it does all makes sense now. In the back of my mind, I wondered how he found me at Spurred that night, or how he always seemed to know how to find me at the resort. Clamping my jaw tight, I approach the desk and close my folder, laying it on top of his mom's file.

Cynthia has sent me a text with a photo attached of a selfie she took of us right before we walked into Spurred.

Cynthia: Forgot I snapped this. Was taking pics of the gorgeous sunrise this morning and ran across it. You still up for that walk on the beach?

Me: Yes! Give me three minutes to change. I need to clear my head.

Cynthia: See you in a few.

Seven minutes later, I approach Cynthia on the beach while she's taking pictures of the rising sun reflecting off the ocean. Of course she looks like she just walked off a nautical magazine with her brown boat shoes, cropped white pants cinched by a soft dark brown belt and light navy blue and white striped boat neck shirt. Her chic style definitely makes me feel plain in shorts and a tank top.

"Capture any good ones?" I slide my hands into my shorts' pockets and rock on my heels.

She smiles and tucks her phone away in her purse, then points to the dark clouds off in the distance. "That storm will be here soon. I wanted to get some pics uploaded to my SnapShots account before it blows in. All my friends are drooling over the ones I've taken so far. Did you have a good evening?" she asks, raising her brows suggestively as we turn and walk along the hard-packed sand.

Squinting against the sun, I stare straight ahead. Even though the wind's starting to pick up already, I'm glad the beach is so quiet this early in the morning. Other than a couple kids playing in the surf, we have the beach to ourselves. "It started off that way." *But I'm not so sure any more.* "How about you? Is Dan still your number one man?"

"He is." She beams. "I'm going to visit him in Maryland next weekend."

"Whoa, so it's serious, then. That's good, right?"

Hiking her purse high on her arm, she slides her hands into her own pockets and shrugs. "I think so. We'll see. So what'd you do last night?"

I stare ahead, my attention snagged on the boathouse at the end of the beach with its bright teal-colored door and red walls. The colors definitely draw the eye. Must be newly painted. "I went on a dinner cruise."

"I suppose it's good you had a nice last meal," she says in a light tone.

Her comment is so odd, I glance her way. "Last mea—?"

A cloth is shoved over my nose and mouth, its sickeningly sweet smell muffling my words. I try to jerk back, but Cynthia grabs me around the waist and grates in my ear, "It's about damn time I finally got you alone. That stupid pilot kept hogging all of your time."

I struggle against her hand, my lungs filling with something awful and wrong, but whatever she put on the cloth—chloroform?—is already working. My legs turn numb and her arm cinches tight, holding me up just before everything goes black.

CHAPTER SIXTEEN

Sebastian

I take a long shower and spend extra time shaving to give Talia space to look over the documents. I hope to hell that's what she's doing and not thinking about what she overheard. Regan showing up was an unexpected complication.

I know that whatever is going on between us is tenuous. Not because I plan to walk away, but because I'm pretty sure that, at any moment, Talia will. All because the idea of exploring our deepest desires in every way possible scares the hell out of her. That and a past I know she's still holding back.

Sex has never scared me. It's raw, pure, and honest. And a lot better without all the bullshit emotions people drag into the mix. My time with Talia has been the most naturally primal experience I've ever had with another woman. I can't seem to get enough of her. Maybe it's because I didn't get her out of my system three years ago, but I've thought about her ever since. Near-fucking-obsessed about her, actually.

And now that I've tasted Talia's sweet body again, I still want her with just as much savage lust. Even now my balls ache while I'm thinking about her. That should scare the shit out of me, but oddly it doesn't. I know I feel relaxed about this because I'm a twisted bastard. Talia will most likely end us before I get a chance to blow up what we have.

That's my specialty, leaving a wake of destroyed relationships and people wherever I go. No amount of money has ever changed that fact about me. Being a SEAL forced discipline on me where it counted for a while, but unfortunately, the military couldn't save me from myself. I'm even more screwed up than the guy Talia met three years ago. He might've had a glimmer of hope for something more with her, but I'm half the person I was back then. Learning to reengage in life, while pretending to be whole has been hard enough since I got back.

For now, I'll enjoy what Talia and I have while we have it. I won't let her pull away from me. I meant what I said; she's mine to keep for as long as it lasts. Hopefully I won't fuck it up before I can help her get past whatever that sick bastard, Hayes, did to her. Then at least one of us won't carry around ghosts for the rest of our lives. Before our time here ends, I'll get his full name from her. He might be in jail, but I grew up on the streets. Between my current contacts and the not-so-legal ones from my youth, that son-of-a-bitch will pay for what he did to her. I'll make sure of it.

Thoughts of Talia draw me out of the bathroom. I tell myself it's because I want to see if she's come up with anything useful in the files I gave her. The truth is I don't want her thinking too long about Regan. The last thing I want is her getting cold feet. We've come a long way and I can't help but hope to build on the trust we've created so far.

My steps slow when I walk into an empty room. Frowning at the blue and beige folders I see on the table, I approach with my chest tightening.

She found the folder I had on her. Fuck. Picking up her phone she'd left behind, I push the button and immediately see a note she typed out on the display.

I left my phone for you. It'll be much easier to track it if it's in your room.

It's bad enough you had me investigated, but then not to tell me when I pointblank asked you if you'd ever tried to find me? I don't know which pisses me off more: the fact that you invaded my privacy, or that you didn't do anything with the information you had. Either way, my response is the same.

Fuck off!

"Goddamnit!" Closing her note, I curl my hand around the cell phone, shaking with the urge to throw it against the wall. Instead, I set the phone on the desk and walk over to the room phone to dial her number.

When her phone rings and rings, then goes to the Hawthorne voicemail, I slam the handset down and quickly change into jeans and a T-shirt.

Grabbing my keycard, I start to head out to track Talia down when her phone buzzes with a text. I pick it up, hoping it might be from her. As soon as I push the button to light up her screen, a text from a friend, Cass, shows up.

Cass: How's it going, girl? Haven't heard from you. Is that smexy pilot keeping you busy?

I smirk. If she's been talking about me to her girlfriend, maybe I haven't royally screwed this up.

Once her friend's text disappears and the phone's background image of a group of people dressed in New Orleans style party garb, smiling and waving around a dinner table, pops up, I set it back down on the stack of folders on my desk. Maybe I should give her some time and it'll occur to her that I did look for her. She never looked for me. Shouldn't that count for something?

Sticky notes poking out of the edge of a few folders draw my attention. I flip the folders open and scan Talia's notes. But it's when I reach the third folder where she has circled several things on the guy's background that I sit down and read Talia's comments about the valet Tommy Slawson.

Spoke to him at the pool and outside the sauna.
He gave me towels and water bottles each time.

She'd also circled the New York home address he lived in as a child and written *"Lower East Side"* next to it. I skim through the background data on Tommy Slawson. No father listed. His mother, Brenna Slawson, died several years ago. No criminal record. Not even a parking ticket.

Talia had circled that Columbia University had been his prior employer, where he'd worked for the main office and the theatre department. "Good catch," I murmur, reading on.

She'd also put a sticky note on the headshot picture I snapped of him laughing at something another Hawthorne employee said. An arrow pointed toward his face and Talia had written "familiar?" beside it. That would make sense if she'd seen him in passing on campus.

Talia's phone buzzes again with another text from Cass.

Cass: You there? I'm jonesing for some Pilot
good stuff. Don't keep me in suspense.

I pick up the phone, intending to have a little fun with her friend, but as soon as the text disappears, I stare at the background picture.

Frowning, I send Talia's background picture to my email, then quickly move over to my laptop to fire up a high-powered facial recognition software.

As soon as the scan is complete, I clench my fists. "Son-of-a-motherfucker!"

CHAPTER SEVENTEEN

Talia

A stinging sensation burns my face at the same time my head snaps sideways. I gasp and open my eyes to see Cynthia leaning over me, her blonde hair dangling in my face.

"It's about time you woke up," she calls over the wind howling outside the salty-smelling building we're in. "You know you really *should* drink more water, Talia. That's probably why you were out longer than I expected. I want you awake for this."

Whatever I'm laying on, it's hard. My face still stinging from her slap, I try to sit up, but my chest and thighs are tied to—I turn my head to see—an upside down flat-bottomed canoe. My gaze darts to take in the space. Surfboards and various one or two man boats and other swimming equipment hang on the walls around us. We must be in the boathouse. "Please let me go, Cynthia. Why are you doing this to a friend?"

"Friend?" Throwing her head back in a deep-bellied laugh, her gaze locks with mine. "I was *never* your friend. Becoming your best bud was a means to an end." Her voice is different now. Definitely harsher. Angry. Vengeful.

Is Cynthia the serial killer? I thought the suspect was a man. As fear for my life whips through me, I try to keep my voice steady even though I'm shaking on the inside. "What do you want from me?"

Instead of answering, Cynthia sets her purse on another boat stacked on a holder next to her and opens it. When she pulls out a pair of rubber doctor-style gloves and starts to put them on, I start screaming as loud as I can.

"Scream all you want." She raises her voice to be heard over me, the thunder, and sand rushing against the building. Pulling a small vial of red liquid from her purse, she continues, "Everyone's inside right now. Probably already drinking and partying it up on the last day of Hawthorne's singles' events. You won't be joining them, of course."

I scream a few more times, then let my voice die out. I may as well save my lungs for running if I can wiggle my way out of these ropes she's tied around me. Cynthia's so blasé, her utter calmness freaks me out more than if she just railed at me. Panicky, I clench and unclench my hands, and when my fingers brush the knot next to my right thigh, I still my hands. *The knot!* I slowly move my hand to cover it.

Distract her. Keep her talking while you work on the knot. "I don't understand. I've only been nice to you. What did I ever do to you?"

"What did you do?" She gapes at me for a second, then lets out a trilling laugh. "You *seem* sweet, but..." She pauses, her blue eyes narrowing to angry slits. "I know how evil you can be. I've felt the sting of your hand, the burn of your curling iron, the spikes of a meat tenderizer, the deep bruising of a belt buckle...basically anything you could get your hands on. And when that didn't work, you made sure I got to experience the darkness of the closet. So yeah, I know firsthand just how vicious and cruel you are."

Cynthia's eyes glaze over while she spews her anger. But it's not me she's looking at. She's looking beyond me, her mind wandering in the past. "That wasn't me, Cynthia. I'm sorry for whoever hurt you, but it wasn't me—ow!"

She grabs a handful of my hair and yanks hard, her crazy eyes spearing right through me. "It was you! He left me because of *you*. Abandoned me to your evilness."

"It wasn't me. *I* didn't hurt you. Was it your mom who hurt you?"

"What? You don't recognize me?" She sneers, then reaches up and yanks hard at her hairline.

I suck in a gasp when her long hair pulls away. The cap underneath comes next, revealing short sandy-blond hair. After she peels off her fake eyelashes, she wipes her lipstick off on her sleeve. When she turns fully my way, Tommy Slawson's face stares back at me, his voice turning deeper. "Do you recognize me now, *Mom*?"

My heart rate jacks and my breathing ramps. "How did you—"

"I become who I need to be," he sneers. "I borrow, steal, kill…whatever it takes to meet my goals, Mom. Goals! Something you told me I'd *never* have."

"Look at me," I say. Even though I know he's off his rocker, I try to reason with him, because self-preservation can be its own desperate form of crazy. "I'm your age. There's no way I can possibly be your mother. I'm *not* her, Tommy."

Hearing his name seems to snap him out of his hate-filled haze. Tommy shakes his head and scowls, folding his arms. "How do you know my name? I never told you."

I blurt out the first thing that comes to mind. "I saw you at Columbia."

Worry fills his expression. "But I was so careful. You didn't see me. You didn't! I made sure of it."

As soon as it occurs to me that Tommy must've been the stalker I thought I imagined in college, he starts to pace, muttering to himself. "He told me to follow you. To find out if you were the one who wrote that article that ruined everything."

He halts and turns back to me. "But when I saw you for the first time, I knew you were more. Honestly, I was glad

I didn't have to write those notes and deal with slipping packages in the mail anymore." He lowers his voice, his eyes traveling over my face. "You were so much more than he ever knew. So I lied and told him you didn't write it, even though I knew you did."

Notes in the mail? Oh God, Tommy must've been the one who put the drug packages with the drop instructions in the students' mailboxes at school. "How did you know I wrote it?" I whisper, realizing that the "he" Tommy's referring to had to be Professor Jacobson, the man who blackmailed his students and ran the whole drug operation at school.

As Tommy moves closer, suddenly all smiles, I try not to shrink back from him. The last thing I want to do is set him off. He's too unstable. I can't imagine it would take much to send him over the edge.

Stroking my hair reverently, he says, "I knew you wrote that article, because I read everything you wrote. The cadence of your voice, your word patterns, they were there if anyone took the time to read them like I did. Even after college, I followed your career at the Tribune and then moved on to your books."

"My—" I swallow to keep my voice from cracking. "My books?" When he looks at me this time, I see the shy guy who handed me towels and water bottles these past few days. Oh God, now his comment about me drinking more water when I first woke up makes sense. He most likely drugged those water bottles with the same stuff he must've put in my beer at Spurred. If it hadn't been for Sebastian, Tommy would've gotten to me long before now.

He nods. "I'm a huge fan, *Miss Lone*. I even joined your fan club. Following your career helped me stay focused for a while."

A sudden dark cloud floats across his calm features as he reaches in his pocket. Pulling out a knife, he flips it open, his voice turning angry. "But then you gave the Hawthorne trip to Delia. That should've been mine!" Clenching his hand around the knife, he jabs the blade into the side of the canoe, rocking it under me.

I bite back my scream of terror while tears of relief silently trickle down my temples.

"So I took care of the old bat," he continues as if the knife isn't currently jammed just three inches from my head. "And it all worked out, because I discovered where you liked to relax, Talia. Here at Hawthorne, I knew I'd get my chance to be alone with you eventually."

I swallow to keep the rising terror locked inside and try to sound calm. "And Mr. Sheehan?"

Tommy smirks, smugness settling on his features. "He thought he could take over the club once Delia died." Bending close, he speaks next to my ear. "No one was going to have access to you, but *me*. Period."

A heavy layer of guilt for Delia and Bradley's deaths slathers on top of my fear. God, Tommy's so unhinged! He can't decide if he despises me, worships me, or thinks I'm his mother. One thing I know for sure. He hates her memory and has marked me as his punching bag for his abused childhood.

Distract him! Redirect. "Why don't you let me go and we can talk books all you want."

"Now why would I do that?" Barking a pleased laugh, he steps back a little bit and begins to unbuckle his belt. "All the fun's about to begin."

"Please, Tommy!" I beg and shake my head frantically as I struggle against the rope. I've almost released the knot on the bottom rope. I just need to yank a little harder.

He pauses for a second, confusion in his face. "Oh, you thought I was going to..." Wrapping the leather end of the belt around his hand, he laughs. "You need to know what you did to me. You need to feel what I felt."

Before I can say anything, he whips the belt around and slams its buckle against my hip. I scream as pain splinters through me, sobbing, "Please stop, Tommy. I'm not your mom."

As he rolls the belt back up once more, he pauses and looks directly into my eyes. "Oh, I know that. I'm punishing *you*, Talia, for all the pain you caused me. You're responsible for everything that happened to me."

This time he hits the belt high on my thigh. I try to curl inward to soften the blow, but I can't move. All I can do is moan through the pain.

Excitement fills his features. He smiles then leans close once more. "The next one will be on your bare skin. That's when the real fun begins. The sight of your blood is what will really do it for me. The pleasure of it spewing everywhere." He jerks his chin toward the bottle he set on the boat behind him. "Know why I bring that?"

I shake my head, hoping he'll stop, but I know he won't.

"When blood dries it turns dark. I want it to stay red, Talia. I want it bright. As bright red as it always felt to me when my own was spewed everywhere!" he finishes on a hateful hiss.

Straightening, he calmly unrolls the belt. "But you won't be alive for that part. That's the after stuff." Stepping close, he slips his belt around my neck. I struggle against the bindings, begging him to let me go, but he puts his mouth against my cheek, his jaw holding my head in place as he slides the leather through the buckle. "I consider it my own special signature."

When I feel the bindings on my legs finally start to give, I attempt to slide my legs off the other side of the canoe, hoping the shift in my weight will free me, but the rope around my chest continues to hold me in place.

Just as Tommy grabs my legs to keep me on the canoe, the sound of the door handle rattling jerks Tommy's head up a second before Sebastian calls out, his deep bass overriding the howling wind. "Talia!"

Grabbing the knife, Tommy jerks back and cuts the rope around me just as the heavy metal door swings open.

Sebastian enters the room, handgun raised, his voice calm and deadly. "Let her go, Slawson."

Tommy pulls me in front of him and jams the tip of his knife against my throat. He laughs and presses the blade just deep enough to pinch. "Back off right now or I'll jab this deep. How will you save her while she's bleeding out?"

Sebastian doesn't blink. He remains perfectly still, his focus only on Tommy. "Release her or die."

Chuckling, Tommy shifts behind me even more, using me as a shield. I can barely feel my arm where he's squeezing it so tight to hold me in place. "She's everything. The whole reason I'm here. I'm not giving her up. She has to die."

Sebastian shifts his bright blue gaze to me. I see the question in his eyes. I've seen it before. *Do you trust me?* I hold myself perfectly still and slowly close my eyes.

The single gunshot deafens me, and I feel the bullet whiz past my cheek before it slams Tommy back into the stack of boats behind us.

Sebastian hauls me into his arms before Tommy even hits the floor. "Fuck, that was close," he whispers harshly against my temple.

As I stare at Tommy's unmoving body, I know he's dead. Sebastian's sniper skills assured that. "Are you talking about the bullet that came with an inch of my face or the fact I almost died?" I ask in a shaky voice, lifting my hand to the belt around my neck.

Sebastian slides the belt off for me, then turns my face toward his, his voice a rough rasp. "I'm talking about how close I came to losing you. I'm sorry, Talia. For everything."

Knowing we still need to talk, I nod. "How did you know where to find us?"

He snorts and shakes his head. "Your shrewd mind helped me piece it together, while your stubbornness saved your life."

When I raise my eyebrows, he nods. "It's true. If you hadn't left your phone behind in my room, I wouldn't have known where to start looking. Your phone had all the info I needed to connect Cynthia to Tommy."

"It did? But I didn't connect Cynthia to Tommy. How did you?"

"Your notes on Tommy's folder, the background picture of that fan club event on your phone, and Cynthia's text and selfie with you was all I needed to head toward the beach, where thankfully the impending storm hadn't fully erased your tracks leading here."

"Okay, so that's how you found us." But when I pause and eye him skeptically, he shrugs.

"I did have some great facial recognition software that plots the entire face. Tommy making himself a geek girl in your club was ingenious. The long straight black hair and glasses definitely threw me off, but he didn't change the structure of his face. The software saw past his disguise. And if he played a woman once before, he could've done it again. That's how I matched his face to Cynthia's."

I stare at him, a bit awed that he figured it out. "But I still don't see how you even thought to check the photo on my phone?"

He flashes a confident smile. "Where had Tommy worked at Columbia? Do you remember?"

"He worked in the main office and the theater

department." I let out a half-laugh. "The theater…that must be how he learned to disguise himself so well."

"If you hadn't highlighted his employment at Columbia in your notes, I might not have looked twice at his background there."

I grimace. "It turns out you were right about our cases crossing too."

"They did connect?"

Nodding, I tell him how Tommy was involved in the drug ring I stopped back in college.

Sebastian rolls his shoulders. "I thought it was crazy that the two cases could be connected, but the overlaps just felt too coincidental."

"Tommy had to have been the redhead who paid Hank to buy that Hawthorne voucher." Sighing, I blow out a relieved breath. "At least it's over."

"Not quite." Sebastian sighs. "We still have to go over all this with Simon and the police. Are you ready?"

When I nod, he pulls my phone from his jean pocket and dials.

CHAPTER EIGHTEEN

Talia

After a whole day spent at the police station, including a quick dinner of pizza while signing tons of paperwork, I'm exhausted by the time Sebastian and I reach the resort.

"I feel like I could sleep for a week," I say as I lean against the elevator wall and close my eyes. "At least I don't have to be back until later tomorrow night. I can sleep in."

Sebastian grunts and pushes the elevator buttons. When the bell pings, I open my eyes and frown when I see we're on Sebastian's floor. "I'm on five."

"Why don't you stay in my room? You can take a shower and go to bed early if you want."

I tilt my head. "I can do that in my own room."

"Do you really want to be alone tonight?"

No, I don't, but I also don't have the brainpower for a battle of wits with you either. "I'm all questioned out right now."

Just as I lean over to push the button for my floor, Sebastian captures my hand, his eyes searching mine. "Do it for me, Talia. I almost lost you today."

The concern in his voice melts my heart, so I nod and follow him to his room. Once we walk in, I say, "I'm grabbing a hot shower to wash off all the sand."

When I start to move away, Sebastian's fingers lace with mine. Rubbing his thumb over mine, he says softly, "What made you angrier? The fact that I invaded your privacy, or that I didn't do anything with the information?"

"Both made me equally mad."

His gaze searches mine. "I only bugged your phone to know where you were at all times. I wasn't taking a chance that I might've missed something and you were still in danger."

"You should've told me."

His mouth presses in a stubborn line. "I don't regret the time we had together without the case getting in the way, Talia."

The emotion reflected in his voice softens my anger. I don't either. And if he hadn't bugged my phone, I never would've been pissed enough to leave it in his room in the first place, and I'd be dead, so his instincts weren't off. When I nod and he starts to smile, I add, "Just don't ever do that again."

I move to pull away, but he holds fast. "What did I say to you when you wouldn't tell me your name that night at the party? Do you remember?"

"I remember you chose my body over my name," I say, smirking.

His expression hardens. Releasing me, he walks toward the desk, saying over his shoulder, "While you're in the shower, try to remember."

I take an extra long shower, doing everything I can to scrub the experience with Tommy from my mind and body.

While I blow-dry my hair, my gaze locks on the pearls for the hundredth time since I walked in the bathroom. Sebastian had returned them to the hand towel where he'd found them this morning and apparently hadn't touched them since.

The answer to Sebastian's question pops into my head as I'm finger-combing my hair into a tousled style.

Sliding back into my underwear, tank-top, and shorts, I open the door and step out of the steamy bathroom, saying, "I remember—" But I cut myself off when I see him sitting on the end of his bed, elbows on his knees, his watch dangling between his fingers. I step closer and touch his bent head. "Is everything okay?"

Sebastian sets the watch on the bed and stands to cup my jaw, his blue eyes tracing my face like he's seeing it for the first time. "That was you that night eleven years ago?"

My attention snags on the white box and my note sitting on the desk next to the open brown box. He said it was stuff from his sister. Guess she finally found the box and sent it. Blinking back tears, I nod. "I was telling you the truth the night of the party. I was Red."

"I *knew* you recognized me." He shakes his head, frustration flickering as his thumbs trace my cheekbones. "Why didn't you tell me we'd met before?"

I clasp his wrists, my heart racing. "For obvious reasons, I don't talk about my past."

Frustration reflects in his eyes, then his tone softens as he trails his knuckles over my cheek. "That's where 'rainbow' came from, isn't it?"

My face flushes, full of heat. "It's the first word that popped into my mind. I'm glad you finally got your watch, Sebastian. At least now you know your father really did care and was proud of you. I wanted you to have it back as soon as possible, so you could start working on mending things with him. I guess three years late is better than never."

He snorts. "I never went back to the Hamptons house. And giving something to Mina for safekeeping…let's just say you haven't seen her room when life is going well. I'm surprised she can find herself in there."

"Why didn't you do anything with the information your investigator collected on me?"

He releases me, his hands falling to his sides. "I just wanted to know you were okay. Don't look at me like that. You didn't meet me at the coffee house. Nor did you try to find me."

"I knew you weren't going to hang around." When he frowns at me, I smile and place my hand on his chest.

"But I'm glad to know I was wrong about you. You're definitely someone I can depend on."

Sebastian visibly stiffens. "I'm not that person, Talia. I'm a lot of things: a protector, a defender, I'm fair and bluntly honest, and yeah, I'm fucking good in bed, but I'm not always going to be there."

I step back, his words hitting me hard. Every man in my life has abandoned me in some way or another. Sebastian isn't like any of them. "I know different."

He shakes his head, his jaw tightening. "No, you don't."

Why does he seem angry? "Yes, I do. At least you used to be someone to depend on," I say, glancing at the end of the bed.

He frowns and points to the watch. "Are you talking about that? Slipping that watch in your pocket back then was a reckless, youthful mistake. One I can never take back."

Mistake? He read the note I wrote. How can he not know how much his words hurt me? "You know what, I'm suddenly very tired." I pivot and head for the door.

Just as I start to grab my purse, he turns me around, his hands on my shoulders. "Where are you going?"

"I'm all talked out for the night."

His brows pull down. "We're not done talking."

I raise my chin, my heart pounding from anger, and hurt, and other emotions I don't want to think about. "I think we've said enough."

His expression hardens and his fingers tighten on

my shoulders. "You're right. Let's do what we do best." Before I can respond, he jerks me close and plants a searing kiss on me that sends a jolt of molten desire firing through my body.

Just when my hands uncurl by my sides, he sets me back against the door and flattens his palms against the wood on either side of me. "I'm going to give you one chance to walk out this door." His piercing hunter's gaze slides over my face, down my throat and then back up. "Know this, if you stay, I'm not holding back. You'd better be damn sure before you use your safe word. There'll be no crying wolf. Not tonight." He inhales next to my neck, a low, primal groan vibrating deep in his throat. "Punishment will be torturous."

I've never seen such an intensely hungry look in his eyes before. My body wants him with a fierceness that scares me, but my mind is rebelling, telling me to leave before he fully captures the one thing I can't protect from him, my heart.

As if he knows I'm waging an internal battle and half out the door already, Sebastian kisses me just behind my ear. "We're fucking fantastic together." His lips make my skin prickle while his deep voice slides hotly through my veins like a smooth top shelf whisky. "That's one thing you can't ignore or debate or talk yourself out of. What we have is a primal connection. Give us free rein and let it burn."

Maybe he's right. If I let whatever this is ignite between us tonight, maybe it'll be like a comet, burning hard and fast, but will fizzle out. At least then, I'll no longer feel this strong gravitational pull to his forceful nature.

Sebastian slides his hands away from the door and takes a step back, waiting.

My breathing ramps as I match his steady regard, but can I really stay with him another night? This sexy man, with his black hair, arresting blue eyes, and sinful smile, makes my heart thunder like it's trying to break out of my chest. Will tonight change us?

He said he can't be depended on to be there. I need someone who will.

I grab my purse and open the door, but the handle yanks out of my hand when Sebastian forcefully pushes it shut at the same time he aligns his chest with my back. "Don't leave, Talia," he says, pressing his lips to my hair.

His wrecked voice shatters my resolve. Sebastian is the type of man who never has to beg. That's probably as close as he'll ever get. The fact that he's breaking his own rules is enough to lock me in place.

When he wraps a strong arm around my waist, his hand pressing me back against his hard body, I release my purse and let it fall to the floor. Digging my fingers into his hair, I tug him closer as his lips slide along my throat.

"You drive me crazy, you know that," he says, sounding annoyed and aroused at the same time.

"Right back at you," I say, then gasp when he pulls my tank top off and makes quick work of my bra.

As both pieces of clothes fall to the floor, Sebastian

removes his shirt. I hold my breath when his hot chest meets my back and his palms slide down my chest. "Remember when I made you come while standing?" he says, his voice velvet smooth as his fingers pluck at my nipples.

I don't trust my voice not to come out like a squeak, so I nod.

His low chuckle sounds in my ear. "Do you want to be standing this time around too?"

I quickly slide my hands down his hips and across the front of his jeans, gripping his hard erection through the thick material. "Do you?"

Grunting in my ear, he turns me around and lifts me in his arms to carry me to the bed in two swift strides.

"Are you in a hurry, Mister Black?" I tease as he lays me down on the bed.

Reaching for the button on my shorts, he undoes it and the zipper in record time. "On the contrary, I'm just laying the table. Fine dining needs to be served with just the right accouterments." He tugs my shorts off in one swift movement, then pauses when his gaze lands on the raised red welts on my hip and thigh that have started to turn black and blue.

The anticipation thrumming through me dims at the look of fury on Sebastian's face. I capture his fisted hand and uncurl his fingers, placing them on the edge of my underwear riding my hip. "It looks worse than it feels. I'm fine, Sebastian."

"I want to shoot that crazy bastard all over again,"

he snarls as he tenderly runs his fingers over my welts. His pained gaze shifts to me. "I'm sorry I didn't get there sooner."

I shake my head. "Just help me celebrate being alive. The rest will heal."

A wicked smile tilts his lips. "That, I can do, Little Red." Instead of ripping my underwear this time, he gently slides it down, periodically stopping to kiss erogenous areas on my leg along the way.

When he prowls back up my body, then kisses my bellybutton before standing, I watch him slide out of his jeans and underwear, my eyes straying to his perfectly muscled ass as he pulls a couple things from his nightstand.

I sit up on my knees as he steps toward the bed. Tracing my finger down the goody trail of hair low on his waist, I slide my hand around his cock and pull him toward me, smiling.

He's frowning slightly, which makes me laugh. "What? Don't you want me to taste you?" I ask right before I dip my head and wrap my lips around the very tip of his erection.

A rush of harsh breath gusts out before he grips my hair in a gentle hold. "I'd love that, but—" His words cut off on a deep groan when I trace my tongue around his sensitive tip.

As soon as he pulls out of my hold, he hauls me up and against his chest, his mouth and tongue plundering mine with dominant thrusts. Pulling back, he puts his forehead to mine. "Fucking hell. You never cease to blow me away…and I do mean that in the best way possible."

Giggling at his pun, I glance down at the black bits of cloth in his hand. "What's that for?"

A dark, salacious look fills his gaze. "I bought this just for you. Lay back and hold onto the headboard spindles."

When I start to say something, he jerks his head back and forth twice. "Don't argue, Talia. This is for you as much as it is for me. Understand?"

Nodding, I lie back. As I grab hold of the wrought iron spindles and watch him tie the black cloth around my first wrist, I say, "Go a little easy, okay? I'm still a bit sore from last night."

When a Cheshire grin spreads across Sebastian's face, I jerk on the second binding he just finished tying. Crossing my legs, I hook them at the ankles. "Hmm, I think I'm closed for business tonight, since you seem a little too amused at my expense."

"Closed for business, huh?" Sebastian clasps my chin and kisses me hard. Biting my bottom lip, he chuckles as he pulls back. "God, I love your sassy mouth."

I frown, determined to keep my legs locked in place. "I'm serious."

He traces a finger down my nose and along my chin, then under my jaw, trailing past the hollow in my throat. "We'll just see if we can't get you to open up, maybe even have a fire sale, hmm?"

He's such an arrogant smartass. "Ha, good luck!"

Sebastian gives a deep, pleased laugh. "Oh, I intend

to be the most persuasive patron and best customer ever. Shall we get started?"

I narrow my eyes slightly, not trusting his jovial attitude. "Enjoy trying."

"Oh, I will, sweetheart," he says just before he reaches over and ties another black cloth around my eyes. "There," he says, tugging the cloth down so it covers my eyes completely, but doesn't impede my nose or breathing at all.

It's tight enough that it doesn't move, but I can see clearly through the intricate black lace. "If your goal was to blindfold me, I think you got shafted on the material. Seems to be a lot of that happening to you lately. Maybe *you* need a keeper."

"You can see me, right?" When I sigh that he seems unaffected by my jabs and nod, he leans close and whispers in my ear, "You're about to find out why I'm the master of your rainbow, Talia."

As the meaning of his words hit me, Sebastian quickly straddles my hips, but doesn't sit his full weight on them. Instead, he slides his hands slowly up my arms, starting at my wrists, then traces his fingers down along the softer underside of my arms.

I try not to react to his touch, even though it feels so intimate and personal. When he reaches my face, he leans forward and nips at my earlobe before gliding his hands along my jaw, his lips following at a leisurely pace.

Pausing at my throat, he touches my necklace. "That night you had two hearts on this chain, didn't you? Why is it so important to you?"

I swallow at the sudden sadness his question evokes. "I did have two, but the other heart went to a better place, representing a promise I made in Amelia's name."

His gaze snaps to mine, sympathy in the blue depths. "I'm truly sorry you lost your sister."

"And I'm sorry you lost your mom in such a horrible way."

Brief pain reflects in his eyes before he nods.

Bending, he kisses each collarbone tenderly, then he moves down my chest. "Do you remember what I said to you when you wouldn't tell me your name that night?" he asks in a husky voice right before he drops a kiss on the curve of my breast.

"You said you'd just call me yours," I say, trying to keep my voice steady.

"Hmmm, you are *mine*," he grates out in a possessive tone at the same time he lifts my breasts together. He dips his nose between the cleavage he's created, murmuring, "This is my second favorite place on you."

"Second favorite?" I ask, trying not to let his words get to me.

He lifts his head, eyebrows raised as he slides his thumbs across my nipples in an erotic drag. "My favorite place is currently closed for business, but—" Pinching my nipples, he smirks as I arch into the pleasure and pain he's inflicting. "I'm thinking I see movement inside. Some lights turning on, maybe."

He rolls my nipples between his fingers with just

enough pressure to make me gasp as hard throbbing slams between my thighs. Just when I start to squirm, Sebastian commands, "Spread your legs."

"No way!" I shake my head back and forth. "That'll make it too easy for you. I'm not giving in."

He tugs on my nipples, then rubs his thumbs on their undersides. I gasp, enjoying this new erotic sensation I've never felt before. "*Now*, Talia. It's not a request," he says curtly. "I promise not to touch you until you're begging me to."

"Fine!" I huff and spread my legs, already missing the bit of friction my thighs provided.

I also kind of miss seeing Sebastian's gorgeous eyes and body with my vision unimpeded, but this noir-ish view is also pretty damn sexy too. I definitely feel everything more intensely this way, since my shrouded viewpoint seems to make me focus on what's right in front of me instead of letting me be distracted by everything else around me. I'm sure that was Sebastian's intent in making me wear the mask. He wants to be the center of my attention.

Bending forward, Sebastian takes a nipple deep into his mouth and sucks hard, pressing it against the roof of his mouth. I groan and nearly come off the bed, I'm so aroused and wet.

He lifts his head, giving me a knowing smile. "Are you ready to turn that lock and throw open the doors yet?"

I shake my head, even though I'm trembling.

Sebastian's nostrils flair. "I smell your arousal, Talia. Its sweet aroma is waving at me like a red flag. Are you sure?" he prods, twirling my nipples with wicked, merciless mastery.

I put my feet on the bed and arch my back, so on edge that I nearly buck Sebastian off. Even though he's having fun at my expense, I'm determined to outlast him.

When he suddenly gets up and walks into the bathroom, I call after him, smugness in my tone. "Are you giving up so soon?"

He comes back into the room, washcloth in hand, his hard erection bouncing against his muscular stomach with his confident stride.

"What are you doing?" I start to shut my legs, but he shakes his head.

"Keep your legs where they are and trust that I'm a man of my word."

His expression is so serious, I ease my legs back open and shriek at the cold cloth he presses against me. "That's freezing!" I grit out, even as I allow him to hold it on me.

He nods. "As it should be. You're sore because you're swollen. The cold will help take the swelling down." After he tortures me with two more rounds of freezing compresses, Sebastian approaches the bed, dark eyebrow raised. "Feel better?"

"I don't know. I can't feel anything down there right now, since I'm numb. Guess this store's not opening due to icy conditions."

"You just need a good thawing." Chuckling, Sebastian

puts one knee on the bed and leans forward to breathe warm breath against my body.

"That's cheating!"

When I try to squirm away, he holds me in place, his grip firm. "Stay put. I promised I wouldn't touch you and I won't." His blue eyes lock with mine. "But feel free to let me know when you're sufficiently warmed up."

He moves close to me again, sharing his warmth and driving me crazy all at once. A couple minutes later, I'm squirming and trying to accidently bump against his mouth in the hopes he won't be able to resist staying right where he lands. Not that I would ever admit that to him.

"I wanted you to tell me your name willingly, Talia. That's what I said to you when you refused to tell me your name." I'm surprised he's going back to our earlier discussion, but I wait to hear what else he has to say. "That's why I never let my investigator look into your past before the time that I met you. I wanted you to tell me. For you to want to fill in the blanks."

"Sharing goes both ways, Sebastian," I pant out when his mouth accidently brushes against me. "That alarm on your watch has something to do with your mother's death, doesn't it?"

He hooks his hand under my thigh and sets his chin in the bend of my leg.

"It's not in that report, but the police tried to accuse my mother of dealing drugs or some other illegal activity because I said she had a cell phone in her nightstand that I didn't know about." His hand on my thigh tightens. "I had to listen to those assholes say that's probably why she got shot."

He didn't answer my question about the alarm he sets, but he shared *something*. Afraid to push too hard, I ask, "Do you know where the phone came from?"

He nods, running his cheek along my thigh. "My dad. He told me later that once Mom found out no more could be done to save her life, she went to him and told him about me. She wanted to know that when she died, I wouldn't be alone. That's when he gave her the phone."

I push my thigh against his jaw, touching his face the only way I can. "He didn't know about you?"

He slowly shakes his head. "My guess is she was afraid he'd try to take me away from her. She'd been so wrong…"

The bitterness in his tone makes my heart ache. "He told you how he felt about you on that watch, Sebastian."

Sebastian's only answer is to kiss my belly, his grip tightening on my thighs before his mouth moves lower, his deep voice rumbling so close to my sex I can almost feel his mouth. "You are so beautiful." He releases a low groan, his focus locked on my wet sex. "I'm a starving man, cruelly teased by this gorgeous spread of Talia laid out like a five-course meal."

"There's so much about you I don't know," I say, trying to get him to open up more.

"All I can do is stare and imagine your tasty flavor and how good it feels to thrust my tongue deep inside, making you wetter. And how much I enjoy it when your juices are sliding down my throat, all sweet and musky, ripe with want. For *me*," he finishes on a desperate growl. When his eyes lock with mine, the look of unadulterated hunger in them is my undoing.

"You win—" I start to say, but Sebastian's mouth is already on me, his thumbs spreading me wide, his tongue thrusting, then lapping greedily. Swallowing, he goes in deeper, taking me. All of me. I'm so primed he doesn't even have to slide a finger in my channel. The second his hot mouth lands on my clit, my orgasm roars through my whole body in powerful, near painful contractions. The experience is so surreal I see colorful flashes of light behind my tightly closed eyes. Every color of the rainbow, damn his talented mouth. I grip the bindings holding me in place and push hard against his mouth, demanding more and loving every second of what he masterfully gives.

When I stop moving and lay there panting through the explosive experience, Sebastian moves up and unties my wrists. Sliding my mask off, he clasps my waist and rolls onto his back, tugging me with him. He presses his lips to my jaw, then pulls me fully on top of him, his voice hoarse with need. "Fuck me, Talia."

We both moan in unison as I slide down his erection. Sebastian's hands grip my hips tight. I can tell he wants to direct me, so I lean forward and press my breasts to his chest. "Show me how you like it."

His gaze flares with heat as I sit back and let him fill me up, taking me fully. "God, you feel so damn good.

Just move, sweetheart." As I rock my hips, then gyrate them in a circle, Sebastian's neck muscles strain, his hands locking on my hips. "Fuck! Everything you do feels amazing."

When he surges upward, I gasp at how deep he goes, but then I move to repeat the pleasurable motion as my channel starts to tighten. "Everything *we* do feels amazing," I breathe out just as another orgasm takes over my body.

Sebastian pistons into me hard and deep twice more, then roars his pleasure as his orgasm washes over him.

I collapse onto his chest and rub my nose along his skin, soaking in his wonderful smell. I'll never get enough of it.

Sebastian rolls us onto our sides, his hand gripping my hip to keep our bodies connected. His breathing still heavy, he runs his nose up my throat, satisfaction in his tone. "I'm fine staying like this all night."

When our breathing settles, he rubs his thumb along my cheekbone. "Tell me about that night I drove you home. Were you running away because of Hayes?"

I start to turn away, but he cups my head and holds me in place. "Tell me."

I slowly exhale a calming breath, my heart thudding. "That's the night Amelia died."

His hold on me tightens. "What happened?"

I keep my gaze on his, because I know if I close my eyes I'll see the whole scene in my head all over again. Just like I have hundreds of times before. "Walt killed her." At the look of shock on his face, I continue, "He didn't mean to kill Amelia, but he could've prevented it. That sweet little girl meant everything to me."

"How did he *accidently* kill his own child?" he asks in disbelief.

I can't say any more. I just...can't. I shake my head and a tear escapes.

Sighing, he rubs the moisture off the bridge of my nose. "No more talk about the past tonight."

I nod and press my face into his chest as he slides his fingers into my hair.

When I hear his breathing even out after a few minutes, I remember how little sleep we'd gotten the night before. Pushing back a little, I lay there, fighting sleep as I stare at his long black lashes resting against his gorgeous face. I can't believe how, even something as simple as that about him, draws me in. He looks so approachable while he's sleeping.

Why is it that the only time you ever try to open up to me is when we're in bed, Sebastian? And even then, you only share so much, choosing to mostly remain in the shadows. I know why I hold back, but what's your story? Once again, I've been shadow fucked. But damn, you sure are excellent at it.

I reach over and touch his jaw, studying his appealing features, memorizing them. *I respect and appreciate so much about you, but most of all your blunt honesty, even when it hurts. I wish things between us were as simple and easy as snuggling in bed all night, but knowing that one day you'll just be gone isn't something I'll be able to handle.*

CHAPTER NINETEEN

Sebastian

I roll over and blindly slide my hand to capture Talia, intending to pull her into my sleep-warmed embrace, but my fingers meet cool sheets. Jerking fully awake, I lift my head and call out toward the bathroom. "Talia?"

When she doesn't answer, I jump out of bed and poke my head in the door. Empty. That's when I notice her clothes and purse are gone too. "What the fuck?" Jamming a hand through my hair, I dial her room, but she doesn't answer.

Frustration mounts as I step into my clothes, but then I finally notice the note she left for me on the desk.

I can't thank you enough for having my back
these past few days. I wouldn't be here without

you. I appreciate everything you've done, from helping me face past issues to building some new memories to last beyond a lifetime. And now you're off the hook. I took the early ferry back so you could sleep in. Take care of yourself, Mister Black.
Always fondly,
Scarlett Red

Crumpling the paper into a tight ball, I toss it across the room, grating out, "Why the hell did she leave?" She said she didn't have to be back until late tonight. We could've had the whole day together. What did I say or do that upset her? I dig my fingers into my scalp and pace, trying to think back. I could tell she didn't want to talk any more about her past, so I didn't push her last night. The only time she appeared upset with me and walked away was when I talked about the watch. But why?

One person might have a clue. I stop pacing and open up my laptop. Clicking to open the video conferencing software, I dial Mina's email.

"So this is what you look like when not in a suit or uniform," Mina teases as soon as her face pops up on the screen. "I kind of like the scruffy you."

Scrubbing my hand against my overnight beard, I stare at the gold floating heart on her necklace. "I knew I'd seen it before."

Her brow furrows and she pushes a hank of blonde hair behind her ear. "Seen what?"

I nod toward her. "The heart on the necklace you're wearing. Talia gave it to you, didn't she?"

My sister's brown eyes widen. "She told you her name?"

"You knew it all along?" I ask, scowling.

Mina touches the heart. "We made promises to each other that night, Sebastian. The heart was supposed to be given to her sister who died. She said my coloring reminded her of Amelia and that it was nice to see what it would've looked like on her had she grown up. Talia made me promise not to reveal her name and in return she'd keep my name out of the article she wrote." Pausing, she smiles. "Did you get the package I sent? Talia brought the box by for you the next morning."

The fact that Talia didn't show at the coffee shop but went by the house really pisses me off. I grind my back teeth and try to stay focused. "It would've been better if I'd gotten it before three years had passed, Mina."

Mina's face turns red. "I'm sorry, Seb. You know how messy my room can get. I put the box away so it wouldn't get thrown in the trash by accident. Then I completely forgot about it until I had to clean my room out for Mom." She doesn't miss a beat before asking excitedly, "Well, what was in the box?"

"You don't know?"

She shakes her head. "'It's a rainbow' is all Talia said about it when I asked."

I hold up my wrist. "It's the watch I lost when I was seventeen. The one your mom accused me of hocking."

Mina winces. "Mom can be such a bitch when it comes to you. How did Talia happen to have your watch?"

I shake my head. "It's a long story. Is that all Talia said when she gave you the box?"

Mina nods, her blonde brows pulling together. "Was there a note or anything inside?"

I nod and lift the note from the desk. "Yeah."

"Well?" Mina spins her hand in a fast circle. "What did the note say?"

I'll never forget Isabel's surprised look when my father yelled at me about losing the watch. It was as if she didn't know he'd bought it, but she sure jumped on the fact I'd lost something so expensive. I'll bet she didn't know he'd had it engraved on the back either. If I show this to Mina, she'll give her mom hell. Sure wish I could be there to see Isabel's face. I turn the note around so Mina can read it herself.

"Hold it steady," Mina orders before she reads it out loud.

> I think you might've forgotten what rainbows look like, so it's my turn to show you exactly where to look. I have a feeling you never saw the inscription on the back of this. Read it and know that he loves you. He's proud of you. Remember, family always forgives.
> Take care, Blackie.
> Red

When I start to set the note down, Mina fusses. "I'm not done reading it. Put that back up!"

I snort and drop the paper. "That's it. That's all the note said."

Mina snaps her fingers. "Sebastian Quinn Blake, put that note back up so I can read it. There was a P.S. I want to see the rest of what she wrote."

Shaking my head, I lift the letter and read exactly what she just read to me. "That's it. The only P.S. going on is your pregnancy syndrome."

Mina rolls her eyes. "If you don't put that note back up right now, I'm going to crawl through this screen and choke you."

"Those hormones are really kicking in, aren't they?" I chuckle and hold the letter up for Mina once more.

P.S. You have no idea how much having this meant to me. Once I saw the message on the back, I couldn't sell it, but knowing the watch was there, the comfort and security it provided was all I needed to keep putting one foot in front of the other. Thank you for the rainbow.

I rip the letter back around and stare at the page, then crumple the paper in my hand, muttering, "Fucking hell!" No wonder Talia got so upset. I told her that giving the watch to her was a reckless mistake, one I couldn't take back. And yet that watch had meant *everything* to her.

"You gave it to her that night, didn't you, Seb?" Mina

asks. "You gave it away thinking that she might need it. That's exactly something you would do."

When I nod and exhale a harsh breath, my sister's blonde eyebrows pull together and she quietly asks, "You looked right at the paper and were adamant nothing else was there. Did you not want to acknowledge that last part for some reason?"

I un-crumple the note and stare at it as I jam my hands into my hair. *How can I make this right with Talia?* "I just can't read it."

"Don't tell me you're one of those anal-retentive guys who only believes in black ink," Mina's says, her tone turning snippy. "So she wrote that last part in green. Big deal. It's the message that counts."

Grabbing a fistful of my hair, my gaze snaps to hers, frustration and anger exploding inside me. "No, I literally can't fucking read it, Mina!"

Stay tuned for BLACKEST RED (IN THE SHADOWS, PART 3)!

If you found **SCARLETT RED** an entertaining and enjoyable read, I hope you'll consider taking the time to leave a review and share your thoughts in the online bookstore where you purchased it. Your review could be the one to help another reader decide to read SCARLETT RED and the other books in the IN THE SHADOWS serial!

To keep up-to-date when the next **IN THE SHADOWS** book will release, join my free newsletter http://bit.ly/11tqAQN . An email will come straight to your inbox on the day a new book releases.

Other Books by
P.T. MICHELLE

In the Shadows Serial (Contemporary Romance, 18+)
Mister Black (Part 1)
Scarlett Red (Part 2)
Blackest Red (Part 3) - TBA

Brightest Kind of Darkness Series
(YA/New Adult Paranormal Romance, 16+)
Ethan (Prequel)
Brightest Kind of Darkness (book 1)
Lucid (book 2)
Destiny (book 3)
Desire (book 4)
Awaken (book 5) - TBA

Other works by
P.T. MICHELLE
writing as
PATRICE MICHELLE

Bad in Boots series (Contemporary Romance, 18+)
Harm's Hunger
Ty's Temptation
Colt's Choice
Josh's Justice

Kendrian Vampires series
(Paranormal Romance, 18+)
A Taste for Passion
A Taste for Revenge
A Taste for Control

Scions series (Paranormal Romance, 18+)
Scions: Resurrection
Scions: Insurrection
Scions: Perception
Scions: Revelation

To contact P.T. Michelle and stay up-to-date on her
latest releases:

WEBSITE
http://www.ptmichelle.com

FACEBOOK
https://www.facebook.com/PTMichelleAuthor

TWITTER
https://twitter.com/P.T.Michelle

TUMBLR
http://ptmichelleauthor.tumblr.com/

GOODREADS
https://www.goodreads.com/author/
show/4862274.P_T_Michelle

PINTEREST
http://www.pinterest.com/ptmichelle/

Sign up/join P.T. Michelle's:

NEWSLETTER
(free newsletter announcing book releases and special contests)
http://bit.ly/11tqAQN

FACEBOOK READERS' GROUP
https://www.facebook.com/groups/376324052499720/

GOODREADS READERS' GROUP
https://www.goodreads.com/group/show/130689-p-t-michelle-patrice-michelle-books

ACKNOWLEDGEMENTS

To my fantastic beta readers: Joey Berube, Amy Bensette, and Magen Chambers, thank you so much for reading *Scarlett Red* so quickly and for giving honest and truly great feedback. I'm so happy you loved this one so much. You all have definitely made *Scarlett Red* an even better story.

To my fabulous critique partner, Trisha Wolfe, thank you for reading *Scarlett Red,* for your invaluable critiques and the brainstorming sessions. You always rock, girl!

To my family, thank you for understanding the time and effort each book takes. I love you all for your wonderful support.

To my fantastic fans, thank you for loving my books and for spreading the word by posting reviews and telling all your reader friends about them whenever you get a chance. I appreciate all your support!

ABOUT THE AUTHOR

P.T. Michelle is the *NEW YORK TIMES, USA TODAY,* and International Bestselling author of the New Adult contemporary romance serial IN THE SHADOWS, the YA/New Adult crossover series BRIGHTEST KIND OF DARKNESS, and the romance series: BAD IN BOOTS, KENDRIAN VAMPIRES and SCIONS (listed under Patrice Michelle). She keeps a spiral notepad with her at all times, even on her nightstand. When P.T. isn't writing, she can usually be found reading or taking pictures of landscapes, sunsets and anything beautiful or odd in nature.

To keep up-to-date when the next P.T. Michelle book will release, join P.T.'s free newsletter:
http://bit.ly/11tqAQN

This paperback interior was designed and formatted by

Made in the USA
Columbia, SC
11 April 2023